She Ca

To Chris & Bill —

With warmest regards, and my good wishes always, to the finest of friends,

Neal

March 25, 2003

# She Came of Decent People

*A NOVEL*

Neal Holland Duncan

BookSurge, LLC

# She Came of Decent People

...Who knows but the world may end tonight...
...I'd hoped she would love me. Here we ride...

**The Last Ride Together**
Robert Browning

*In Memory of*
*Ruth Ashley Walde Lightfoot*
*There is no greater treasure than a real friend*
*and*
*Margaret (Mrs. Henry Clinton Mackall)*
*who also graces these pages*

# Chapter One

*Except to admit I was eight months shy of my fiftieth birthday,* I shall remain nameless. So shall she of whom I write. She who came of decent people. I was in the library, the last of the houseguests who Rsvp'd acceptance to Nesta Parry's oversized invitation requesting white tie, decorations and diamonds to a dance at *The Squirrels,* Nesta's oversized house outside Philadelphia in Chestnut Hill. The sun made the outside appear warmer than it was. It was the open fire that provided the room's real warmth and the scent of burning applewood that prevailed. Nesta uncrossed her elegant legs and walked to the tall windows. The curtains were edged with green ball-fringe, yard upon yard of it and looped back with green silk ropes, each ending in a foot-long tassel. She peered out at the drive, impressive with its mature oaks and copper beeches. The way her ash blonde hair was cut defined her classic bone structure. A frown broke her serene profile, "Wherever can he be?"

'He' is Bud, an Irish leprechaun of advanced age, who had met me at the top of the escalators of the 30th Street Station and whisked my grips and me into his vintage red Cadillac the morning before. Only Nesta would dare have eight houseguests and forty-two for dinner, followed by a dance on a Tuesday.

"Why be commonplace?" she justified.

Why, indeed?

"You're going to miss your train. I do hope nothing has happened. What a bother," she sighed.

The library furniture gleams like the panelling after a century of beeswaxing, a legacy to a hundred Doras. The house and follied gardens possess a charm that only age can create.

One notices the fresh smell of wax on the polished oak staircase leading up to the guest floors. Cut flowers. Deep upholstered armchairs and peaceful ageless solid furniture.

"There will be another train, Nesta," I comforted. "Don't fret. You know how I love being here with you."

Any response to that was checked by the ringing phone and the daily announcing a girl fresh and impossibly young. Younger than springtime, actually. Something brand new and just out of a bandbox. I stopped chewing the horseradish in my shrimp-cocktail-thick Bloody Mary and Nesta smiled warmly at someone's treasured daughter, as I rose and introduced myself. Something sparked between us, for only a second, before disappearing, but it was there, definitely there. I could hear Nesta saying, "Yes, I do understand. The airport is too awful at anytime and you certainly aren't getting any younger. None of us is..."

That made me wince inwardly because Alice from Wonderland made me feel a thousand years her senior, standing there silent with an eager look in her thick-lashed, green-gray, black-pupiled eyes of the sort that could pull the soul out of a man with their devilment and charm. She gave new meaning to the word gamine. Especially posed the way she was with her toes pointed inward and her hands clasped in front of her swinging a brown wicker basket overflowing with flowers and fruit and dressed by Laura Ashley.

"No, I'll drive him to the train. No, I shan't need you tomorrow. Goodbye. Well, you heard," Nesta sighed again. Replacing the receiver, she reclipped her gold earring as she came to where we were standing and warmly asked, "What have you there, lovely child? Had you been older, or we younger, I would have invited you to my party."

The girl wrinkled her nose but refrained from turning up her upper lip. Instead, she spoke in a clear polite voice. I shook my head and listened to neither of them. I was transfixed by and fixed on her magnificent eyes.

"Mother has talked of little else since coming down to

breakfast, and Father sends you the best from his greenhouse. Perhaps next year I'll be old enough for the grown-ups."

I grinned at that. This girl talked her own language. She was young, vital, untouched. She had courage. Standing by her, feeling the unsaid, I experienced a keen excitement. I saw her desirable and desirous mouth shape the empty words. It was in a way comparable to something I'd once known and thought I'd forgotten. The still undercurrent of almost unbearable sensation. The tightening of nerve and muscle. In ignoring it, I felt like a thief smiling at her.

Made to feel *de trop* by her visitor, Nesta recovered with, "I'm sure you will. Do thank your father for me. Tell him I'll do the flowers myself." Nesta also noticed that I was being regarded with interest. She twinkled, "I can see you 'two' have already become acquainted."

I spoke her name and the sound of my voice was strange to me, "Yes, Nesta, we introduced ourselves."

Turning back to Nesta's guest, I asked, "Are you at Shipley?"

At once her manner changed, taking on that indescribable awareness, that unspoken overlay of recognition and challenge that the predatory female shows when she sights something worth a chase. She had no need of Nesta's murmurings, standing there, provocative and luminous.

"Shipley! I finished Dartmouth over two years ago. I'm past twenty-three and own one-half of a public relations agency."

I narrowed my eyes and my compressed lips broke into my thoughts. "No need to get carried away. I'm not about to tell you the year I finished Sewanee."

"Is that where you learned to talk funny?"

"No funnier than you."

She gave me a mild pout like a child pretending to be sorry.

"What was your major?"

I cleared my throat.

"English."

"Economics."

"Economics!"

After that I was only conscious of the flurry of departing activity that occurred when the 'lovely child' volunteered to drive me to the station. Then being in a black Mercedes as the trees gave way to open road and her asking with a curious sidelong glance, "Is it important that you make the five-twenty-five?"

I moved my shoulders.

"No. Why?"

"I thought perhaps we could have a drink."

She sounded out of breath. I said nothing.

"It was just a thought," she flushed.

She made growing old a tragedy of life. I hesitated before looking at my watch. "There's no reason why we couldn't. The bar at Racquet opens in eleven minutes. Would that be too moribund for you?"

She gave me the briefest stare and a half-mocking smile before adding, "Or chaste enough?"

"Both," I replied seriously.

"The Racquet Club is fine. Father is a member."

"Good, then you know the way."

"Have you been a member long?"

"Quite a while. It's a good place to entertain and convenient. I don't always stay with Nesta."

She gave me a crooked smile. "You get around."

I straightened up. "Ah, yes I do."

"Do you play squash?"

I told her I didn't *play* anything anymore and she asked me to light her a cigarette. Hers was a Camel. I took a deep drag before handing it over. I hadn't smoked an unfiltered cigarette in over twenty years. My toes seemed to curl as the traffic became heavier. Headlights coming on were bringing out the combative natures of the drivers. I noted that she was an aggressive driver and recalled what Cantwell Walsh's mistress said to him before slamming the door behind her. "You're only aggressive in bed or driving. Not in getting a divorce." Was my driver similarly aggressive. Beneath the soft ivory tulip skin and the traces of baby fat along the jawline of the perfect oval face lurked no-nonsense features. I became aware that she was watching me in the long silence of stalled traffic.

"I won't ask you how you keep that tan in November, but it goes well with your blonde white hair, camel's coat and three-button navy suit. I like white shirts and they suit you, especially that one with its rounded collar and gold safety pin."

On that we exchanged looks, and I made a wry attempt at a smile before my slack lines firmed up to positive contours. She pulled at a strand of hair until the driver of the car behind us put pressure on his horn.

Looking ahead, she asked, "Have you lived in Washington long?"

"All my life. I'm a fourteenth generation Virginian/Washingtonian."

She clicked her tongue. "That's a long time."

"Yes, it is. Some would say it makes me a cave dweller."

"Do you have children?"

"None that I'm aware of and no wife either. Anything else?"

She jumped a little. "Were you ever—?"

Was she holding her breath?

"Ever what? Oh, married? Yes, but...but she died."

"Recently?"

"No."

"Did you love her?"

"What an ill-bred question," I chided, with enough veiled mocking to keep her from bristling. "But to answer your question, let's say we respected and appreciated one another. Sometimes that's better than love. Love is a complicated business. Messy sometimes, too. But I have loved. Uncontrollably. Violently. With no thought except for the moment. Unheeding and careless in whom I hurt and ending up hurting myself the most."

We continued on in companionable silence. She parked in the lot on South Sydenham and we entered the club from the back entrance after being buzzed in by the head porter. The heavy door locked behind us and our voices echoed down the cavernous hall, draughty for all its cushioned luxury.

"I've never been here when the club was empty. It's like a great mausoleum. Father would bring me here for the children's Christmas party. I cried when I became too old to even pretend to believe in Santa Claus."

"And, you wore velvet and climbed to the first landing where the marble staircase divides and posed like the little girl in the foreground of Sargent's *The Boit Children*."

For a moment she appeared stunned.

"Besides knowing a lot about art—"

"A lot about Sargent," I corrected.

"All right, Sargent. But how would you know that?"

"Because I've invited children of friends to the same party. You might say I suffer from an *in loco parentis* disposition."

Of the seven men in the bar, one is the bartender. Aged, but erect, and after sixty-two years of service, according to the club bulletin. Next is the waiter who is growing middle-aged while waiting for the old man's death. And, at the center table, a group of four acolytes in investment grey hover on every pontificating word from the mouth of some senior partner. It is on his distinguished head that my guest bestows a smile of such singular magnitude that his distinguished self is quite taken aback.

"What's your pleaseure?" I asked, pulling out her chair. She glanced in the direction of the sideboard, "A wedge of Stilton, no crackers, and a double Stoly. No ice."

I stopped my eyebrows from rising, gave the waiter our order and settled in.

"How old is your father?"

"Sixty-six."

"I'm eight months shy of fifty."

"I didn't ask."

"In other words, when you were born I was twenty-five or twenty-six."

"I don't care."

"I do. I'll never be young again."

That brought a faint smile to her face. Rather abstractly she removed a bit of tobacco from her tongue while continuing to regard me languidly. Our waiter with the embattled smile returned. I sipped my drink and watched her nibble at a piece of the creamy veined cheese. The way her throat moved when she swallowed heightened my frustration. Then like a dash of cold water hitting me came words so softly spoken that I thought of death.

"I wish you would stop treating me as one of your 'children' or a pubescent virgin. I'm not. I haven't been since I was nineteen. The man was sixty-two, an account executive with J. Walter Thompson. And, while I no longer sleep with him, I occasionally see him. I left him for my former boyfriend's father. He's a brain surgeon, and if you say his brain should be examined I'll leave you sitting here."

I think my face fell. I drank thankfully, while stifling an uncomfortable thought about blood loyalty or, more specifically, father-son loyalty, and then looked into her thick-lashed eyes. I felt depleted.

She gave me a defensive glance.

"You're shocked. I'm glad. You believe I should be married to a younger version of yourself, live in Chestnut Hill with two perfect children, a daily, a live-in nanny, and be doing my provisional work for Junior League."

I tightened my lips and began cautiously.

"Besides what I think, there's such a thing as blood loyalty. Forgetting the difference in age, there's the same skin. How can a father's loyalty to a son be swept aside for a hot current in the blood? How do you stoutly deny there's no harm in what you do?"

She looked at the tops of her hands. I noticed for the first time the framed Indian embroidery representing the tree of life.

"I don't. And unless you're above reproach, don't be judgmental."

I shifted in my chair and cleared my throat. The first phase had ended.

"As I thought. So order me a club soda and I'll drive you to Wilmington."

"Wilmington?"

"It's only twenty-five minutes away. You can catch a train there. It will give us more time."

I closed my mind to my conscience as her headlights sped through the night. The ashtray was full. I lowered the window and threw my cigarette into darkness. I hated myself for being sentimental, a man moved by memory and conscience. I was like a Lochinvar in reverse.

"Ever been to Wilmington?"

"Never," I replied with stiff lips and thought, do I want this rash adventure?

"Tell me if you like this?" she asked. "Father and I went to hear him...that's where I saw you! I knew I'd seen you before."

"Saw me where?"

The CD filled the car's interior with orchestral strings.

"At the Academy of Music in April. You were seated in Parquet Circle A. We were on the other side. Luciano Berio was to conduct with Garrick Ohlsson at the piano..."

Perhaps this rash adventure was meant to be.

"...Only Berio became sick and a new program was substituted. You kept going to sleep, but stayed in your seat at intermission, being polite to a dowager that I thought was your grandmother. It was you, wasn't it?"

"It was I. You have remarkable eyesight and an even better memory. Nesta bought my ticket. She has a season subscription. That's why we weren't seated together. I'd caught an early train that Friday. I was up for the weekend. I took her to Delullo's for a long lunch before the two o'clock matinee. After that, we went to a barn of a shop in Society Hill. I forget the name."

"Was it Gargoyle's?"

"That's it! I bought a pre-World War I soccer ball that I didn't need but had to have that came from the playing fields of Harrow. And on Sunday, there was a brunch at *Andalusia*."

"You certainly get around," she commented for the second time.

"You haven't been?"

"No, we don't know the Biddles."

That was odd. Her parents attended Nesta's dance and Jimmy and Cathy had been there.

"What's *Andalusia* like?"

"There's a needlepoint pillow in the drawing room of the dower house that says it all."

"And what is that?"

"God was born a Biddle."

"You're right. That says it all."

She turned down the volume.

"You're very fond of Nesta, aren't you?"

"Yes, I am. Nesta is a rare woman of grace and form with a disposition of perfect harmony."

"Do you prefer older women?"

"I prefer women. But to get back to Nesta, being at *The Squirrels* is like being from a large family or being back at school with all the comings and goings."

"You have everything."

"Not everything. No one has everything."

Only the truly young can think that.

Seeing Wilmington made me glad I wasn't staying over. Downtown appeared abandoned and the railway station a Dickensian place where tough guys from the underbelly rumble about its sooty facade.

"I'll see you off," she said as she smoothly slid into a reserved for handicapped spot with total self-confidence. The parking area was poorly illuminated and mostly empty. I retrieved my things from her trunk and we hurried up the stairs to the platform. In the crisp November night, she breathed energy. Smiling, she angled her face close to mine, "So what do you do when you aren't partying in Philadelphia...or elsewhere?"

Her warm breath on my mouth brought instant response in my loins. She's a cheeky little thing I thought. Still she made my tongue feel thick.

"You really should rephrase that question to 'What do you do when you're not *relaxing* in Philadelphia?' When I'm not *relaxing,* I write. Writing is my living and it's hard work. When I need to get away from it, I relax in Philadelphia...or elsewhere. Satisfied?"

A nervous laugh escaped and heat rushed from her cheeks to her hairline. "I guess," she said, throwing back her hair that was cut to align just past her jaw. I wanted to nuzzle her sweet-smelling hair. Instead I gulped frosty air. Reality seemed fragile, beyond my grasp. Reason was called for but none was present. My brows furrowed. I opened my mouth, then shut it. The breath in my throat burned. I leaned back against the fluted cast iron column and closed my eyes. Raucous male voices sounded behind me. It was enough to give one ear rot. I turned up the collar of my coat. She touched my lips and penitently asked, "What do you write about?"

That made me laugh. I felt indescribable elation. I straightened up. "About growing up in WASP gentility in the age of WASP disintegration."

"Does that stuff sell?"

She did it again, but I let it pass.

"It used to. Very well, in fact. Now the royalties are about played out. My last book didn't go paperback. The money from two movie options is about gone, too. But I would be misleading you if I didn't admit to another source of income. Without which I'd be bad off."

"A trust fund, I suppose."

"Several inheritances, actually. I'm all right so long as I don't touch the capital. I also inherited a house from a great-aunt. A spinster of monumental breeding and character."

"And it's in Georgetown, I'm sure."

I stopped a frown and answered evenly, "Capitol Hill. A flat front Federal two blocks from the Capitol. Georgetown was nothing until Roosevelt brought in the New Dealers. It was they who brought Georgetown back and made it fashionable. Now, my aunt was above everything. When the Hill started to go, she dug in and—"

"I know what those old barracks can be like," she again assumed. "Water in the cellar, termites in the beams, rotten floorboards, cracked plaster-work and a roof like a sieve. I'm sorry for you having such a millstone—" She stopped and mused savagely, "Ooooo, how I must sound. My parents are always on me for my bluntness. But so many of my friends are redoing... I'm going to make a vow to stop impulsive presumptions about anything or anyone."

"It might be advisable, considering my house only needs some paint and a patch on that part of the roof over a back bedroom."

I thought she went into a trance, but I was the one. I noticed how the wind that keened down the track loved her thick dark hair. Her hand turned palm up to smooth an eyebrow. Why so strange and beautiful? She's the sort of person who ought always be young. I wanted to put a string on the moon and give it to her as a balloon. When she spoke again she said, "I'm glad the woman I thought was your grandmother, wasn't."

"Why?"

"Even from where I was seated I could tell she was the type who, if she treats you too kindly, she's thinking of you as a servant. The kind who abounds in Chestnut Hill."

That certainly brought me back to reality.

"You're dead wrong. She was sweet, if a bit dotty. We discussed religion. Her nephew is an Episcopal bishop. When I inquired whether he was a churchman or a dissident she assured me that both he and his wife were well-born."

"What's the difference?", asked with a little less certainty, was her only reaction to a story I'm dining out on.

"You're obviously not an Episcopalian."

"I guess you could say we're Presbyterians."

I touched her cheek and looked hard into her eyes, "I wouldn't care if you were a heathen or a Baptist. Understand?"

She understood just as she knew I wanted to kiss her there on the platform as the train wheezed in with its hoarse whistling and hissing sounds. Nobody would have cared. Meetings and goodbyes were common here. I looked 'round a little wildly, dashed my cigarette, and in a rush of words asked, "Do you ever visit Washington?"

The train jerked to a halt. All along its length people were getting out. I caught her in my arms. I wanted to swing her off her feet. The flush of excitement enhanced her cheeks. I felt heady in the rush of adventure. "How can I contact you?"

"What?" she laughed.

"I said, how can I contact you?"

Breaking away, she fumbled in her bag. "Here, call me at the office."

I looked down at the card.

"Tomorrow's Armistice Day. I'll call you Friday."

A conductor with an undertaker's face nudged me on with, "Train's leaving, Mista." I swung my suit bag over my arm, picked up my grip, and stepped across the threshold. "Friday," I repeated, turning back."

The door sliced between us and locked. She moved forward. I was trying to read her lips through the grimy window and then she was gone.

# Chapter Two

*I was in the best of spirits the next morning. I shaved, smiling at* the card I'd stuck in the frame of the mirror. Dressed in worn gray flannels, a fresh white oxford shirt, and crew neck navy blue sweater, I crossed the hall to the study ready to do any revisions needed on the first chapters of my untitled new book. I didn't need the grandfather clock in the downstairs hall to tell me it was eight o'clock. I was restless as a pony and anxious to get back to my writing.

My house bespeaks solidity and orderly living. I crave the resumption of tactual intimacies that is the essence of coming home. Without this security, I wither, no matter where I am or how fine a time I'm having. I poked at the log fire laid by Danny for the sheer pleasure derived from handling the polished brass poker. The crackle of the fire, the beam of morning sunlight, welcomed me. On my desk, Danny had sorted the mail into invitations, letters, and bills. I noted that there were more bills than invitations. Things could be difficult if my mind stopped working. There'll be no more inheritances. I moved to the window to view the garden in all its autumnal glory. Under the big corner tree was a carpet of yellow leaves. Virginia creeper burned like fire on the high brick walls that separate my property from the adjoining houses. I took in that the red vine over the arch of the faded black door to the old carriage house had the familiar masses of hard little grapes that seldom ripen. And observed that the next rain would scatter the late roses, red, yellow and white, covering the iron gazebo.

Pulling myself away, I touched the familiar tray with the two Thermos bottles of chicory coffee, the plate with three homemade iced sugar cookies, my favorite cup and one perfectly laundered napkin. The tray was in need of replating. So was I, but I sighed at my good fortune. Danny spoils me. Danny spoils everyone. I sat down, lighted a cigarette and poured my first cup of coffee. And, as I do every morning, I glanced at the photograph of Ursula and me. However, this morning, I stopped. It was as if I were looking at strangers who faced a camera filled with radiant youth and bright expectations. Had I ever really looked like that, notwithstanding the hussars costume and plumed helmet that was loaned from a military museum? Had Ursula? The Hungarian gypsy who holds me so tenderly. Am I forgetting us? I have forgotten us. Even the shared intimacies, I think. I know. I turned my mind to the newly returned typed chapters and decided any revisions can wait, as can the mail. I started chapter four and filled the yellow legal paper with black scratchings from a new felt tip pen until the grandfather clock chimed one very precisely. Very loudly. I leaned back and stretched. The coffee and cookies were gone. I went down the narrow backstairs carrying the tray to the kitchen. Its original stone-flagged floor today struck cold through my red-soled, ancient white bucks. I saw Danny's note propped against the covered Stone China cheese dish on the scrubbed-white oak table.

"Don't forget to get your haircut. The Lightfoot party is next Thursday. Black tie."

That's right. Ruth and Philip have arranged this dinner for me to meet the drama critic, Richard Coe.

The kitchen smelled of petunias and ham.

"Dave is closing at one-thirty. Best eat later. He's expecting you."

I thrive on being cosseted.

"See you tonight, Danny. You *are* still eating in? P.S. There's lima beans and ham hock on the stove and cornbread in the oven. I would have made a pie but you worry so about your weight. Missed ya. P.P.S. Call Amanda. Your agent didn't call. Sorry. That woman did."

'That woman' is Calypso Fox. Danny's dislike of her is boundless and abiding.

Danny's tidy and well-tended kitchen comforted me like a womb until an anxious twinge traveled my middle. I wondered about *her.* She who came of decent people. I'm neat. I'm more than neat. I've become compulsive. It's Danny who is naturally neat. I wondered again about *her.* Was she.... I stopped. "Not now," I said louder than I'd meant to to the walls of the low-ceiling beamed room. But I can't. She's old enough to be hurt by me. But am I old enough not to be hurt by her? I stomped my feet. Perhaps I should buy some rag rugs. I wouldn't want Danny to get chilblains.

But what *she* is, is a *menace,* I reflected with a thin smile before rinsing my cup. I sliced a chunk of Swiss cheese to stave off hunger and went through to the front hall to what was once the telephone room under the stairs. At Brooks Brothers' Christmas sale the year before last I'd bought a leather-sleeved varsity jacket that I'd convinced myself I needed and have hardly worn since, owing to my belief that I come across as a caricature of some aging High School Harry or Joe College. This afternoon, however, I didn't care. Thus garbed, I bent and straightened the Ferouz runner that needs retacking before removing my bucket rain hat with the jaunty navy/red club stripe grosgrain band from the staff held by the six foot statue of Diana of the Hunt. My great-aunt would not have been amused. After all, she was the model for the original. So I'm glad the dogs at Diana's feet can't bark. But I feel my hat breaks the formality of the faux stonework walls that rise above the wainscoting. I reset the burglar alarm in the vestibule and winked at the soccer ball on the china elephant garden seat. The fancy mosaic tiled foyer remains as colorful as it was when it was first laid by Italian artisans. Outside, on the Philadelphia-forged stoop, I breathed deeply of the sharply chilled air which immediately brought forth a chesty audible wheeze. Trap has done the boxwood proud. Also, the front door brass blazes like a sanctuary lamp and cobwebs no longer weave across the fanlight. The gas flame in the carriage lights enhances their luster and the matching fluted steel mud scrapers make me itch to have mud on my shoes. Contented, I shut the gate behind me that Trap has not forgotten to oil, snapped up my jacket, put my hands in my pockets and walked briskly the eight blocks to Dave's.

I feel about the Hill the way Samuel Johnson felt about London. And after twenty-six years, the visual feast of every outing is like the first time for me. When I tire of the Hill, I'll be tired of life. Even rushing, I take in everything, especially the Christmas decorations that start earlier each year. Thanksgiving remains a remote thirteen days away. Dave's revolving barber pole is a survivor. So is Dave as the owner/proprietor of one of the last great barber shops. Here, the big chairs pump up and back and Vitalis and Wildroot Cream Oil line the shelves. Dave and I always have a lot of catching up to do. Today, we caught up too much and he mucked up. I could have had Trap cut my hair. He certainly couldn't have done worse. Dave knew I was displeased. I said, "Goddamn," a word I seldom use, to my reflection. He tried to give back the ten dollar bill. Eight for the haircut and two for the tip. I restrained from saying that won't put the hair back on the sides. He rang up the amount in the big National Cash Register, the bell pealed and he said the next two are on him. They certainly will be. On my way back, I reminded myself that I should be thankful for not being bald and that I do have a week before the Lightfoot party to grow hair.

Seeing my house immediately put me in a better mood. It is the grail of my character and hugs my subconscious. The windows glisten and, though the shutters and front door won't go another year without repainting, the house and I know that it is well-loved and tended. In the kitchen, I drank a giant glass of sweet milk, as Danny refers to it, and filled my cracked Winnie the Pooh cereal bowl with lima beans and tender chunks of ham that I garnished with freshly chopped onion. The cornbread in the oven was buttered as I like it, on both sides like my toast. Carrying the bowl and the plate, I went through to the room Ursula loved most. Almost the first thing she had done on our taking possession was to make the dining room the garden room and the second double parlor the dining room. I haven't used that room since she died. It's easier to entertain at the club. Danny's always onto me about it. "All that silver. All that china. All that linen that I take the trouble to air twice a year."

"All that work," say I.

"I do the work. Need I remind you?"

Henry James' characters would have relaxed in this eclectic array of furniture and things, unified by creaking herringbone parquetry and threadbare rugs. What William Morris said, "Have nothing in your house which is not beautiful," abounds here. How many combined inheritances had we gone through following his maxim. We were ruthless. What didn't fit and what we didn't like, we sold. At top dollar, however. Sitting in one of the ladder-back chairs, I ate my lunch. Danny's vase of yellow chrysanthemums and asters added a dash of color to the early eighteenth century gate-leg-table. From where I sat I could look at two gardens. The real one and the painted one. T. Mostyn's *The English Garden,* signed and plaqued, that my grandparents bought in London for sixty pounds, eighteen shillings in nineteen twenty-six now hangs here. I also saw how the sun has diminished the rosy personality of the chintz-covered sofa and chairs, but they will last my lifetime. We'll diminish together but not the roof. I frowned at the crack and stain in the warm olive-green ceiling. I'll have a chat with Mr. Gray next week about selling some Potomac Electric shares. If only the book would sell. I noticed that Trap had moved in the potted palms in my absence, blocking the French doors that had replaced the two windows. That means the purplish and pink heliotrope clusters are gone for the season. I wish I knew where Danny hides the iced sugar cookies that are alloted me at my request. A quick search of the butler's pantry failed, so I went to rinse the dishes and remembered that I promised to buy Danny a dishwasher when and if the book sells. "But where do you plan to put one, Danny?" "In my room or outside, if necessary." That made me smile as I hurried up the backstairs and back to the pedestal desk. It was three o'clock. I had four more hours of work ahead of me.

Just after six I yawned and stretched. I was winding down. My ears cocked for the striking of the dinner gong. Until

Danny came, the gong hadn't sounded since those drawn out family gatherings of my sailor-suited childhood where, in a sea of octogenarians, I was a crown prince. Danny, for some reason, pleasures in using the leather-padded mallet on the saucer-shaped brass bell that swings from a self-supporting bamboo stand in the hall. My ears were cocked but my mind was on *her*. I started replaying the conversation that had had no theme, then stopped and decided to call Calypso.

Calypso Fox has a courtesan's body, Boldini hands and a Psyche knot of tawny frosted hair. I have known her all my life. She was Ursula's best friend. Calypso and I suffer at times from the lay-me-down-and-die sugar blues that can come down on us like a cloud. Recently, she's taken to wearing her great-grandmother's chokers. "The neck is the first to go," she shudders. Whatever, they have only increased her regal bearing. She'll be fifty come June and she's scared out of her mind. She's had three annulments and three divorces. The annulments were to the same man. Calypso had and has hot pants. She eloped at fifteen, sixteen and seventeen and each time the detectives hired by her family tracked them down. After the last time, Eddie gave up. Too bad, because the soda jerk from Peoples was the only man Calypso ever really loved. The others were all for money. And after alimony came AA. We're faithful in our fashion. We both stray but we're always there for each other. Calypso and Danny shun one another. They have since that debacle in the garden when Salley Bowles, Calypso's Afghan Hound, destroyed the tranquility of the afternoon by all but raping Danny. Calypso requires massive amounts of sugar served in the form of lemonade when drying out from a siege of the sugar blues. Five pounds of sugar and twelve lemons to a pitcher of water to be exact and this was what Danny was bringing to us when seventy-five pounds of passionate hound pinned Danny to the wall with a long pink salivating tongue.

Danny, struggling not to drop the pitcher, roared, "Get this farting prize bitch off me before I kick her ass to China and back."

"You idiot," Calypso matched, "any fool can see the bitch is in heat."

"Well, I'm not," screeched Danny, "and if you call me any more names it will be your ass I kick to China, you clothes-horse nympho."

This reduced Calypso to a wailing banshee.

"How dare you! Why I'll have you fired. Do you hear—"

Not likely, Calypso.

"Why, I'm on maps. I've had a tundra and waterfall named for—"

"What your name should be on," Danny spat, "is a kennel and this is not the bitch who should be getting this."

'This' was five pounds of sugar water that smashed into Salley Bowles' yelping face. 'This' is why I sleep at Calypso's. For as long as Danny remains on the premises, Calypso will not darken the door.

I should write about this. Instead, I dialed FEderal 7-2731 and Calypso's husky voice floated through the line from Georgetown.

"Darling, I've longed to talk to you all day."

Only once had Calypso interrupted my writing and that was when her father was electrocuted by a bolt of lightning as he sipped a whiskey sour on the terrace at the Chevy Chase Club. I was with her when her mother died.

"Why didn't you call me when you came in? Were you being naughty?"

"No, I was tired. I...I missed my train and had a devil of a wait for another."

"I've missed you."

"And I you. You should have come. You were much missed."

"It's hard for me at large parties with everyone drinking"

"I know, but I'm so very proud of you. It's been two years—"

"And ten days, four hours and thirteen minutes."

"Do you need me, Calypso? I'll come."

"I know you will. You're the only one who will."

"That's not true."

"Yes, it is. It takes me longer and longer to look like my former self."

"I'm leaving now. I'll spend the night."

"No, darling, I'm fine. Really. Thanks to my glue gun. That's what I've been dying to tell you."

One of the doctors at that well-known sanitarium in Stockbridge, Massachusetts, introduced Calypso to the wonderful world of glue guns when he dragged her off to an arts and crafts class under protestations of "You son-of-a-bitch, I'm paying you a thousand dollars a day and you can't look at me and know I'm not the basket weaving type?"

No, what Calypso Fox was was the glue gun type. Last Christmas she surprised me with an antique silver champagne bucket top heavy with pine cones, nuts, and lace-trimmed, wired-velvet ribbon. I was awed. So was Danny who doesn't even resent polishing the bucket sitting atop the highboy between the windows facing the street.

"The Junior League wants everything I've made for their Christmas show at the Madison. And...you'll die...Erika dropped by to say Little Caldonia wants divvies on anything I make. Imagine, starting a cottage industry at my age."

"You're ageless."

"And you're sweet. Don't you go and die on me. Any word from your agent?"

"'Fraid not."

"Shame you can't write trash."

"Ain't that the truth."

"My dress for the Lightfoots will turn heads."

"You would turn heads in a feed sack."

"Not anymore, darling. I have an early appointment with Derek for the works tomorrow. Actually, the works would include a tumble with the to-die-for Derek but he's gay. Do you think heterosexuals are in decline like WASP's?"

"I've no idea, but I can assure you I'm going to write that down."

"You and only you, darling. I'm glad you're back."

"You and only you. I'm glad to be back."

"You're still sleeping over Saturday?"

"Yes."

"Good, you can tell me all about Nesta's party. 'Night."

"'Night."

Amanda's number rang busy so I opened my mail. There was a letter from the 'Pink'. William Parker Hart III that is. We're closer today than when we were at school, if that's possible. I wished, for the hundredth time, that he and Trudy still lived here. Pinky knows me well.

"I can say with confidence that, had you signed a contract for your 'best' book, you would have called before we left."

I certainly would have.

"If you don't get the news you're hoping for, consider this, it's not like you forget how to write after a certain age. Look at me. Though I used to be a fair to mediocre athlete..."

Ever modest Pinky. He'd been idolized by his contemporaries on and off the playing field where the sun burned his best-boy-in-school carrot hair to bronze.

"...I've long-since hung up the jock. If you do the same to your writing you should have your butt kicked. We didn't have World War II but we've seen changes as sweeping since our shared youth and precious few for the better."

The Pink should take up writing when he retires from banking and I would have called to tell him so had he and Trudy not been vacationing in the Cayman Islands. I blinked several times before trying Amanda again.

"Is this Amanda Rucker? Princess Stephanie look-a-like, well-known Washington model and computer genius extraordinaire? It is? Well, this is your favorite author. I'm your only author? Well, I better be. What do you mean by 'another would do you in'? Am I that demanding? Be abusive. You know it turns me on. Okay, I'll stop. Yes, I've gone over the chapters. No, I didn't make many changes but yes, there are typos. I'll let you be the judge. Seriously, Amanda, I don't know how you do it all. Work all day, type all night. Model and now golf pro. You need a man to take care of you. I didn't know you knew such a word. Why not drop golf and become a candy striper at a hospital? You'd meet a doctor, or at least an intern, or perhaps some lonely old man who'd rewrite his will. All right, I'll mind my own business, but I do worry about you. Yes, I had a great time and yes, I've been very productive. I'll leave the revisions and two-thirds of a new chapter in the hall for you when I go down. Not 'til Monday? When I'm on a roll? No, I haven't heard from my agent. I was only gone two days. I am not being defensive. Well then, lunch with me at the club next week. Any day but Friday, Saturday or Sunday. No, I don't have anyone coming in to sleep over. Would I cheat on Calypso? I had no idea you had such a low opinion of me, Amanda. Come by then for drinks. Well, make an effort. I have an idea for a new book. Yes, you will. You need the money until you find a doctor, lawyer or Indian chief. Yeah, I missed you. What sound? Oh, that. That's Danny's way of announcing dinner. It must be seven. Yes, I am spoiled. By Danny and by you, too. Bye."

I went to wash my hands in the best of moods. Danny will want every detail on Nesta's party so I'll give us a drink. Danny favors sick-sweet sherry but I'll give myself a martini with a gin float, I thought, going down the front stairs as I always do for dinner.

# Chapter Three

*I made myself wait until ten, then grabbed a cigarette and dialed* the number in Philadelphia. The receptionist wanted to know, "'Whom' is calling?"

"Tell her a friend. Her long distance friend."

"But—"

So determined was she on announcing me that I lost patience and growled, "Does she have that many friends? And it's 'who' not 'whom,' miss."

"What?"

"Remember it this way. 'Him' isn't calling. 'He' is calling or 'her' isn't calling but 'she' is."

"One moment, sir," she sputtered.

The voice that came on was cautious. I thought we had passed practical tones. I caught Ursula staring at me. I turned our picture face down the way Danny does Calypso's picture when dusting. Levelly, I said, "I called to invite you down for next weekend."

Her, "Hmm," came first. "Let me look at my calendar. My partner and I—"

"Who's your partner?"

What an ill-bred question on my part.

"My sister-in-law."

"Oh."

For some reason I felt relieved.

"I guess I could drive down following the meeting."

She guesses? I lighted another cigarette.

"Why not take the train?"

"Too expensive."

My eyebrows raised. "Fifty-three dollars? Roundtrip."

"I like the freedom a car affords."

"For a fast getaway?"

"You said that."

My flip, flopped.

"Sorry."

"We'll have to continue this later. I'll call you Thursday to confirm. This time give me *your* number."

"It's Lincoln 4—"

"What? Why, you're just like— Give me numbers."

I flinched with anger.

"Listen, trying to teach me new ways would be like trying to ice a sawdust cake."

There was a moment's silence. I was instantly penitent. Had I gone too far? If I had, she let it pass and declared, "What you are, is eccentric."

"If that means I don't need a poll to tell me how to feel or think, then I am. Being eccentric is a natural form of self-protection."

"You don't say," she laughed, openly.

That mollified me. I gave her my number in the numbers I hadn't known.

"Before you go," I asked, "what were you trying to tell me before the train pulled out?"

"I was trying to find out what Armistice Day had to do with your having to call me on Friday rather than Thursday."

I answered, wondering how iconoclastic she really was. "Armistice Day is a holiday. Businesses are closed, and I didn't have your parents' number or know your father's name. I have no recollection of them from the party."

"You've been sequestered too long writing books. Armistice Day is now known as Veterans Day and it's not a national holiday."

Was she amused or amazed by how that statement may have underlined how solitary I really am? I raked my hand through my hair. I didn't know. I also didn't know whether she was happy I'd called or not. What a study in contradictions she is. "I must go," she was saying. "I'll call Thursday. Goodbye." The receiver clicked softly. A frustrated sigh slipped from my lips. I stared at the black rotary dial and Lincoln 4-0837.

The Saturday of her arrival I woke cold and wet with sweat. I tossed about amid crumpled sheets wondering. Wondering if I would find her changed. Wondering if she would think I had. Wondering what we would talk about. Sharp pains darted through my right big toe. I could feel my goutish foot swelling. My future does not bode well. Not yet fifty and cursed with gout. I got up hoping a long soak would help. It didn't. I seized a cigarette with shaky, wet hands but my reflection stopped me from lighting it. God, while I'd never once been bothered by my hair turning white, salt and pepper pubic hair, which this morning appeared more salt than pepper, is another matter. This is worse than white stubble and a bad haircut. Well, almost. Nothing is as bad as a bad haircut. Hair is the first thing one notices. It's what I notice, anyway. Please God, I prayed, don't let me start coming down with the sugar blues. Not today when it would feel so good to feel so good. Not today when I'll be seeing her in less than four hours. I threw on my robe and went into the study for a drink but changed my mind when I saw the two thermoses of coffee on the tray. Why does Danny think I'm working this morning? Was I that off-hand when I asked that the room once occupied by Ursula and me be prepared and aired for an overnight guest? Or is Danny trying to make me feel guilty by not remarking "Oh, it's going to be an ironed white-linen-sheet-weekend, is it?" I'll take the chapter with me in case she's late.

My week had gone well. On Monday, I'd gotten the money for the roof.

"Need I guess the reason of this visit?" Mr. Gray had inquired with the tempered tartness of an avuncular headmaster.

"Must there be a reason Chet?" I laughed, shaking his hand before sitting down.

His jocular manner never fails to make me feel like an errant freshman. His full name is F. Chester Gray. I call him

Chet but I think of him as Mr. Gray. His office is a jumble of portfolios, files and papers. I couldn't function, much less write in such a rabbit warren.

"Not if you dropped by when you didn't need money," he mocked, leaning back in his leather chair and pursing his lips in amusement. His strong chin equals his firm handshake.

"Be fair, Chet," I matched in manner, "How many times have I asked you to lunch?"

"That's true," he admitted, "but I'm not afforded the luxury of long lunches."

"Rubbish."

He smiled. His white hair is wispy and his blue eyes laugh. He is happy to see me.

"That's true. What's the 'emergency' this time?"

"It's like this, Chet."

"You really don't need to explain to me. It's your money. I'm not your trust officer."

"I know, but I want you to know."

I don't know why myself, but I do.

His brow furrows and he again shakes his head.

"You inherited how many shares of Potomac Electric?"

"I know and so do you. I've sold quite a lot but this is an emergency."

"Isn't it always?"

"Chet, I need the money to have the roof patched."

"Why not get a new one? Patching's not like you."

"Because a new tin roof could run eight to ten thousand dollars. A rubber patch, which my pharmacist and his wife have, will serve the purpose. The leak has reached the garden room ceiling. I've put it off too long as it is. Anyway, I don't live extravagantly—"

"And what you're wearing came from Penney's. You'll always believe there's a pony, won't you."

"A pony?

"Allow me to explain. Two brothers one Christmas morning woke to find only two stockings hanging from the mantel. The older brother sobbed, 'My stocking is filled with manure.' 'So is mine,' the younger brother announced. 'There must be a pony outside.'"

Finished, he again leaned back, facing me like a concerned judge.

His analogy as it applied to me was only partially true. All day Thursday I waited for her to call. Would she come? What time was she coming? The uncertainty gnawed at me through Ruth and Philip's party. Not that they or Calypso noticed, though Calypso had raised a quizzical, well-sculptured eyebrow at my chaste kiss and the waiting Yellow Cab.

"Not staying?"

"Can't. Amanda dropped by newly typed pages just as I was leaving and is coming for them in the morning."

"You're on a roll?"

"Ah...yes, I am and as tempted as I am by you in that smashing black dress. I noticed Coe couldn't keep his eyes off you."

"Or his hands."

"At his age?"

"At any age, men are men."

Yes, we are, I reflected, trying not to feel guiltier and antsy to get away.

I was staring at the ceiling in the dark when the call came.

"Were you asleep?" was her opening.

"No."

"I can't come tomorrow."

I was filled with childish rage.

"Why?"

"We're redoing the campaign."

"Why?"

"You wouldn't be interested."

No, I wouldn't. She's right about that.

"We've rescheduled the meeting to Monday morning."

"I'm sorry."

"Are you?"

"What's that supposed to mean?"

"I mean 'sorry' because the campaign's been scrapped or 'sorry' because I'm not coming?"

"Both. Where are you?"

"At the office."

"It's after midnight. Is it safe for you there?"

"You sound like a parent."

"I'm younger than your parents."

"Yes, you are."

"I could come to Philadelphia."

"No, that wouldn't be advisable."

"But I want...I need to see you."

"Do you?"

"Yes, goddammit."

"Well, then, I'll try to come Saturday."

"Do more than try. I think I'll die if I don't see you."

My voice was ragged.

"Do you mean that?"

"Never been more serious in my life. I've not forgotten how to commit."

"I don't gamble."

"Nor do I usually."

I broke off embarrassed.

"What time might I expect you? I'm not that far from Union Station."

"I'm driving."

I made no comment. Only asked, "Do you know the Hill?"

"No, I'm only familiar with Adams-Morgan and know where the Ritz-Carlton is. The boy I told you about lives in Adams-Morgan."

"Does he have a death wish?"

"No, he's a yuppie."

"You like the seriously successful types?"

"I never really liked him at all or that way."

"I'll meet you in the lobby of the Ritz."

"Will you take me to the Jockey Club? He took me once."

"No, I'll take you— I'll let it be a surprise."

"Don't get the notion I'm easy. I'm wrong for a lot of people but not for you I think."

I didn't know about that.

"I must get back to work."

"Go home. It's late."

"You don't know how badly we need this account. Goodbye."

Like St. Paul, she was not born to charm.

"Wait. What time are—?"

"I'll see you around one. Goodnight."

Spent, I fell asleep.

She was late and I kept having to urinate. It was all that coffee I'd followed with Long Island iced tea. I also felt heavier. My hair, which had been passable for the Lightfoot's, was not today. Perhaps because I'd cared too much. Between going to the lavatory and being filled with confusion by the lack of a dress code required by a four-star hotel, I'd had difficulty getting any work done. I was the only person in the lobby wearing real shoes for one thing. Shell, one-piece blucher plain toe cordovans. In fact, I was the only person wearing real clothes. Best gray flannels, double-breasted blue blazer, a burgundy and white striped shirt with a white collar and a favorite bow tie. My fire engine red knee socks denoted just the right panache. Admittedly, it's been a while since I was in a hotel, but maybe I have been living a too rarefied life.

Sweat popped out on my face when I saw her come up the foyer steps. I admired the way she wore her clothes, the darkness of her hair, the brilliance of her skin. I just wished her effect had been a little less toward simple youth, spotless and fresh with casual carelessness. She hesitated at the top, framed by the marble columns, for a count of three beats so I could take her in. She looked absurdly innocent. When shall she look almost innocent? I was as excited as a callow school boy and tried not to limp walking toward her. She gave me a tentative smile before a river of words rushed out. Rolling the pages, I shoved them into the pocket of my mac.

"I'm sorry I'm late." I shouldn't have come. The project's not finished. I worked all night. I may have to drive back— "

I smoothed my hand across the soft cheek before holding her hands in both of mine, not listening to her.

"It doesn't matter. You're here. I was worried. Now everything is all right."

She appeared embarrassed. She looked around. No one was paying us any mind, though we certainly stood out.

"Where are you parked? I'll follow you."

"I came in a taxi."

She gave me one of her crooked smiles. "Where to then? I'm all yours."

Was she?

# Chapter Four

*"You're taking me in there!" Her delicate features registered* disbelief. "This is why you filled the parking meter with a chunk of quarters! This is your 'surprise!'"

'Here' was Tune-Inn, known to cognoscente as the only place on the Hill to eat or drink. Tune-Inn is to bars what Dave's is to barber shops. Everything about them appeals to me, including Tune-Inn's address, 331-1/2 Pennsylvania Avenue, S.W.

"Trust me," I assured, opening the door and pushing her inside to where the juke box moaned the black man blues. From behind the bar, Tony welcomed me, as his eyes took in who was with me. If not with Calypso or Danny, I'm usually alone. Tony gave me a thumbs up as we passed headed for a booth. I'd like to remind this ex-marine of the age of the young woman with whom he lives.

"We're in luck," I smiled.

"We are?"

"Yes, my booth is empty."

"'Your' booth?"

"Yeah, I have squatter's rights."

"If the owner's a taxidermist," she commented as I took her coat, "someone should tell him that most of what's mounted has the mange."

They do. And the marlins are losing their scales. That's part of the Tune-Inn's character. This and the nicotine-stained walls and ceiling.

"No, the owner is the man behind the bar. His grandfather opened for business in the twenties by throwing away the—"

I was interrupted by Caroline coming from the kitchen with the constant Pall Mall dangling from the red lips that match her upswept hair. Caroline is the only person I've ever known who can smoke, talk, take or bring an order and never drop an ash. She is the only person whose weight never changes. I wish I could say the same. I could until I turned forty-five.

"Where you been hiding? It's not like you to miss a week. Suzie says she hasn't seen you either—"

"Caroline, I'd like you to meet—"

"Why, I had no idea you had such a pretty daughter."

My stomach soured.

"Where you been hiding her?"

I cleared my throat pointedly.

"She is *not* my daughter, Caroline."

I couldn't decide whether my voice sounded strained or defeated. Not that it mattered as Caroline was in no way deterred from her course.

"Well, she's pretty enough to be," Caroline confidently continued. "Let me tell you something, dear. Consider yourself lucky to be this man's godchild. All us girls have a favorite regular but your godfather is the one favorite we all agree on."

I threw my mac in the corner. Caroline has just damned me to death with praise. Defeated, I said, "Will you please stop, Caroline. I'm too old to blush," and, heavy-hearted, sat down. Dimly I was aware of Bessie Smith singing *Go Back To Where You Spent Last Night, I Don't Want You Anymore.*

Caroline held on doggedly and leaned on the table.

"Where you from, dear?"

"Philadelphia," she replied, absently picking at a hangnail.

"Is that right?"

Caroline's ash is now over an inch long. She turned to me, "Who's that elegant lady who comes in here with you sometimes? Not Miss Fox. This one is from Philadelphia, too. Says she lives for our burgers and fries."

"Nesta Parry, Caroline."

"That's the one."

She who came of decent people stopped picking at her hangnail.

"You've brought Nesta Parry here?"

"Several times. She fasts for days to splurge. Many notables eat here, including two Supreme Court Justices."

"And not them nor that Senator from New York wear a bow tie as well as this man," Caroline went on.

I was drowning in her barrage, but I stopped slumping and tried to preen, for on any other occasion I am actually quite fond of Caroline. Her disgruntled face quickly changes to smiles on seeing me.

"The art of the bow tie lies in tying it only once and then having the good sense to live with it for the rest of the day."

I believe Oscar Wilde said that. I do know that he said that a well-tied tie is the first serious step in life. It didn't matter for the kitchen bell signaled an order was ready and saved me from anymore of Caroline. I placed our order fast.

"Bring us the works, Caroline. Along with a Bloody Mary and a double Stoly, no ice."

Caroline gulped, knowing that the Bloody Mary was for me. The long ash broke, landing on the formica tabletop like a punctuation mark.

"You drink Stoly straight, dear?"

Her words died.

"Uh-uh," the green-gray eyes shot upward. She crumpled an empty Camel pack before removing another from her bag. Caroline was stumped by her. She remained bent, her palms, one on each side of the table, supporting her.

"Well, I'll be. I guess I won't be running next door to buy you a Popsicle."

"A Popsicle!" my companion laughed, showing all her good teeth.

Caroline reached between us to put out what remained of her cigarette before replying, "Yeah, dear, we don't serve desserts," and ambled off.

Left with that nonsequitur ringing in our ears, we slowly adjusted our legs under the table.

"Is that part of you or part of me?" I asked.

"Part of me."

Our eyes met and we looked away from one another. We were both thinking of our first meeting and suddenly we were formal. I felt looks being exchanged. I lit her cigarette. She inhaled deeply. I felt her breath when she exhaled to blow away Caroline's ash.

"So," she smiled, "tell me, what's 'the works?'"

I stared at her for a long moment and bloomed under her gentle gaze.

"Two double hamburger patties shaped by hand of the finest ground sirloin to be found. Two large slices of sweet Vidalia onions. Crisp lettuce. Home-grown tomatoes. Real mayonnaise. Sharp, melting cheese. And French fries, the best this side of paradise."

"You should put this man on television," she told Tony, who had arrived with our drinks.

"If you were a regular, you would know that we don't need to advertise. But you're right, if we did, he'd be our man."

"Maybe I'll just become one, too, Tony," she sassed.

"Let's hope so," he winked.

Tony left us and she looked intently at her hands before bestowing that appealing crooked smile on me.

"So what other surprises do you have for me?"

"Do you really want to know?"

She looked up then, meeting my eyes with her own.

"Ohhhh yes."

"All right. I've made reservations at the club for seven-thirty."

"What club?"

"City Tavern. It's in Georgetown. John Adams slept there the night before he was sworn in. Then I thought you'd enjoy a nightcap in the Robin's Nest at the restored Willard Hotel. Of course," I added, "I'm always open to suggestions."

She lifted her glass.

"I'm in your hands. I told you."

No, she wasn't.

She stopped sipping her drink.

"What a paradox you are."

Impatience shot through me. I frowned as I lighted a cigarette.

"You must admit that you don't exhibit contradictory aspects of personality on first impression."

I leaned forward before replying.

"Do not make mistakes about my character. That is the worst and easiest error."

"I like you," she smiled sheepishly.

"Hope you all are hungry," Caroline announced. She placed the oval plates in front of us. Rick's hands were obviously bigger than usual. Between us we had over four pounds of sirloin patties.

"What's a Vidalia onion?" she asked, lifting the gargantuan burger with a delighted smile.

I wiped my mouth with the paper napkin.

"A sweet onion grown and shipped from a place in Georgia. Glennville I think—"

She wasn't listening. She was lost in savoring the first bite. Her tongue shot out to catch the grease running out the corner of her mouth. The telephone at the front rang. Tony answered. I know how his brows waggle when he places the receiver under his chin just before he pushes back his baseball hat. I inhaled sharply and drained my glass without a word. I had no appetite for food. I was in love. I fiddled with a French fry while she drank in the sensations of this new world. The feel. The sounds. The raucous laughter. The specialness of this special place. Then I ordered another drink. I staved off any question of why I wasn't eating by taking perfunctory bites.

"So who's 'Miss Fox?'"

I frowned.

"A woman I know."

"Know well?"

"Well and carnally. Or did you think I was living a monastic life prior to meeting you?"

"I'm sorry."

I looked at her critically.

"No you're not. Not in the least. You're nosy."

She blinked slowly.

"Have you known 'her' long?"

"'Her' name is Calypso. Calypso Fox. I've known her all my life. She's a month older than I. She was the Brenda Frazier of her generation."

"Who?"

"Ask your mother. Brenda Frazier was married to Shipwreck Kelly. Twice in fact."

"You made that up."

"No, I didn't."

"Why didn't you marry her? I mean Calypso."

"It's complicated. She loved somebody else."

"And?"

"And I married somebody else."

"Did you cheat on her?"

"Let's use 'her' name. My wife's name was Ursula. Ursula was Calypso's best friend. But, to answer your question, no, I never cheated on Ursula. I came close once, but Ursula became sick and I respected her too much."

"That's the second time you haven't mentioned love."

"No, I haven't, but respect is sometimes better. To fall in love properly can make you unhappy."

"Really?"

"Really."

I smiled at the conceit of the young. She clicked her tongue.

"So, how long have you and Calypso—?"

"Since her last divorce."

"How many times has she—?"

"Three."

"And when was the last?"

"Sometime after Ursula died. Now listen. She has her house. I have mine. We respect the other too much to discuss any quiet indiscretion. By this I mean, we are faithful in our fashion. At the finish, predictability is reassuring."

She smiled vaguely, "When do I get to see this house of yours? The one with the leaky roof."

That pleased me. That and the fact that she'd remembered about the roof.

I had her approach the street from the end where no elms were missing. Where only pieces of sky break through. From here, the matching rows of aged red brick loomed substantial but not massive. Dignified. Restrained, they are. Fashioned for a world that was supposed to endure for those who believed in God, family, good works, parties, receiving and calling. I reflected that the mirroring small-paned windows were at their best at this time of day as we coasted to a stop in front of what is mine.

She switched off the motor, looking up at the house. I slid over the brown leather seat very happy. "It's a decent house. Neither prison nor palace, but a decent house."

There was no response. She only opened the door and remarked before sliding out, "This was never a street for mongrels."

I clamored, "What's that supposed to mean?"

"Nothing. Will you help me with my things?"

I did as she asked, carrying the nylon garment bag and medium sized grip into the front hall.

"Danny will be along soon to take your things up and settle you in."

She stood by the pocket doors. Her dark-lashed eyes contemplated me.

"What did you expect?" I joshed, "Crocheted antimacassars?"

She said nothing.

"Ursula used to say everything in the house married well."

She said nothing.

"I guess you could say it's a fusion of styles. Or a collision," I went on, trying to fill the uncomfortable silence.

She stared at the Chinese Chippendale mirror sitting on the white marble mantelpiece. Ursula's citrus-yellow walls have mellowed well.

"Let me show you through. Our families had a passion for collecting. Mine even more than Ursula's. I've ended up the caretaker."

She spoke at last.

"What's that woman wearing?"

She left me and walked to stand in front of the seven-foot portrait that hung horizontally over the sideboard in the dining room. The painting she saw reflected in the mirror.

"Seven yards of pearls."

"Who is she?"

"Aurora Starr, my great-aunt, who willed me this house. She was named for the Goddess of the Dawn. To artists, she was known as Lucky Starr. She lived off their oxygen. Laszlo, who painted her twice..."

"Who?" she quizzically cut in.

"Laszlo, a contemporary of Sargent. He wrote that there was an intoxicating melange of fire and gentility about Aurora Starr. Her eyelashes would catch in her veil they were so long. It was seductive. Even when she was old. I've never forgotten. By the way, she never posed nude. The painting is an illusion. Only the imagination suggests nudity. Yes, she's lounging on a chaise but the wings and the arms actually hide the forbidden parts. The pearls undulate over a body whose middle torso was actually draped in a rather smelly horse blanket. Aurora was very outspoken and a highly original dresser and thinker. Her obituary stated that she possessed the majestic air of Aida entering the dungeon until the day she died."

"She never married?"

"No, she kept a salon for artists and died a virgin."

"It's in the blood," she commented.

"What?"

"Those contradictory aspects of personality."

"I suppose it is," I answered sincerely, as she proceeded without me to the garden room. I followed, saying, "Ursula delighted in this room. She made it her own. It was once the dining—"

"Who is Danny?"

"The person who takes care of the caretaker and everything else around here. Why?"

She frowned and hurried to peer out of the French windows.

"Nice garden."

I hate the word nice.

"And you have a coach house. Lucky you never have the bother of parking."

"Lucky if I owned an automobile. Calypso thinks it would make a perfect pout house—"

"You don't own a car!" she almost shouted.

One would have thought I'd said I didn't wear underwear.

"Not for a long time," I nodded. "Too much trouble. Anyway, Danny lives in the quarters above and drives a Cherokee country jeep. Time-called taxis work very well. Cheaper, too. My grandparents never owned an automobile. They would call in their respective schedules every morning—"

She cut me off with, "How long has Danny lived out there?"

I couldn't decide whether she was without doubt the most ill-bred person I'd ever encountered or not. However, I held my tongue and replied, "Since just before Ursula died."

She regarded me curiously before asking, "Where do you write?"

"Upstairs. I have a study. We can go up through the kitchen."

I heard the exclamation mark in her voice as we entered.

"This is where you work!"

"Yes, I spend more time here than anywhere in the house. Before the walls of Jericho came down this was two bedrooms. That's why there are two fireplaces."

Her eyes travelled round the room.

"What a lot of books. I suppose you've read them all. Can...May I go up the ladder?"

Quite taken aback, I said, "What do you want? My books are not on the top shelves." But she only replied, "I like ladders. Don't you?"

The thought had never occurred to me. I stared dumbly while she seized the mahogany library-ladder from its corner, planted it against the shelves and ran up as nimbly as if it were a mast to a crow's nest. She stood at the top, holding by the edge of the cornice, peering about, nose to nose with a bust of Sir Walter Scott. She rocked to and fro surveying my domain and ran her fingers along the calf-bound histories that smelt musty up close. She then came down, dusted her hands instinctively at imaginary dust for there was none, and asked with a practical air which sat oddly with her demeanor, "There wouldn't be a computer hidden somewhere among all these 'things?'"

"'Fraid not. I do all my work in longhand. When I have a pile, I leave the pages in the hall for Amanda, my typist. She lives about a mile away and has a key."

"To everything?"

"To the front door," I flatly squelched.

"Do people just naturally spoil you?" she asked without hesitation.

"Perhaps," I replied intently.

"You are truly 'sui generis.'"

And she had impressed me by knowing that Latin phrase. Not that I was planning to compliment her.

"Would you prefer I be ordinary?"

With face averted she gazed determinedly at the photographs of vanished generations that fill the tables. Tablescapes, I think of them, of lean, handsome, beautiful, distinguished, stout, clever, regal and even faintly common individuals unknown for the most part now except to me.

"Well, would you?" I repeated.

She clicked her tongue and shrugged philosophically, "I don't know. I really don't know. I know I love the smell of old leather in this room."

At my desk, she fixed her eyes on the silver-framed photograph of Calypso.

"Who's the vamp with all the kohl around her eyes?" she smiled, her mouth a straight line that didn't divide.

"Calypso. Calypso Fox." I answered too quickly.

"Ursula is...was exquisite. You obviously..."

"Obviously what?"

"Obviously enjoyed one another."

"We did."

She gave me a sidelong look.

"How old is Danny?"

"The same age as I, but what is this thing with Danny? If you have any more questions, I suggest you direct them to—"

Danny's fortissimo voice rang up from the hall, "I see she's here. I'll be right up with her things."

She who came of decent people stiffened markedly as Danny entered, fast and easy, wearing green slacks and a black wool sweater with a thick cowl collar coming up to the ears. Clear barrettes held back pale blonde hair that showed through the white and gray. She had on her favorite gold hoop earrings and new penny loafers.

"Danny, this is—"

"I know her name," she laughed in her pleasant offhand way, "you've told me at least a dozen times this week."

My guest's eyes gaped and stared blankly. Like a china doll whose eye mechanism has suddenly snapped.

"You're Danny!"

"I am."

"But I thought—?" she stumbled.

"Thought what?" smiled Danny.

"Thought...I thought you were old," she managed with a smattering of grace.

My mouth twisted bitterly. Like Hell. I know what she thought. Slow though I had been.

"I'm ancient compared to you," Danny laughed with amusement. "Come let me show you your room. It's the loveliest in the house and hardly ever used. It was theirs." Danny shot me an accusatory glance, before departing. "And Miss Starr's before that."

"Everything should be in a museum," I heard Danny telling her. "That chaise is the same one Miss Starr posed on. The artist with the funny name, he gave it to her. On the bad days I'd carry Ursula from the bed and put her there. I'd start a fire even on a hot day and take one of her lovely brushes and stand by the hour brushing her beautiful hair. She had hair like yours only blacker. Like sable it was. There were those who said she dyed it, but she didn't. I know. After she was embalmed I went and dressed her and did her hair. They weren't going to let me. You could have heard him at The White House. He told them it was what Ursula would have wanted and he wouldn't pay the bill unless they let me in the back. Later, when I've turned down the bed, I want you to look closely at the sheets. Irish linen they are. Embroidered by the nuns and slyly mended by me. I handwash, starch, and iron them myself. Do you like sugar cookies with vanilla icing? There are some there under the napkin on the table by the bed. I bake them when he's away. They're his favorite. I have to hide them. Would you like me to light a fire?"

I wished myself elsewhere and tried to shut my ears to their jangling voices. The bedroom is not that far away. Only across the hall. I felt an interloper. To drown them out I limped to the console and put on a stack of Eddy Duchin seventy-eights and then to the footed drink tray kept on the false drawer of the William IV or Adams breakfront that pulls out to become a desk. My hand shook as I reached for the decanter containing vodka.

*Shine on, Shine on Harvest Moon* was playing when my guest returned, to tell me that Danny had shown her my bedroom. I handed her a drink and stared at her miserably. Miserably because it's the last time for love and I wanted more. Needed more. Not a one-time fling no more meaningful than masturbation. Miserably because I'm too old to want May when it's December. Miserably because I know how well my compartmentalized life suits me. No surprises. A social routine that only changes with the season. But watching her made me lonely. Lonely for the kind of happiness that belonged to youth. Lonely to love again. Lonely to share for the first time since...Well, had she come for a fling, we were both going to be disappointed.

She ignored my look and deadpanned, "Nice dog painting," before going directly to the tufted leather Chesterfield where she curled with feet tucked beneath her, melting into the down cushions. I trailed and sat down in one of the matching wing chairs to the left of her and looked at her blankly. She regarded me over the rim of her glass. The fire ebbed.

The 'nice dog painting' was a massive Victorian oil of two German short-haired pointers. Not that I cared. But why are we bandying words? Sparring as it were. I wanted to say, "Tell me you're happy to see me." "Tell me you like my house." "Tell me you like my tie," even. But most of all, "Tell me at least you like me and explain why I need someone like you to love?" Instead she remarked on my bedroom:

"What a quiet little room you habitate. It's almost Spartan in its military orderliness."

The sanctum of my room is austere. 'Prussian,' Calypso claims. But I deigned not to reply. My face only clouded when she mentioned Danny.

"You should tell Danny not to wear so much eyeliner. She has the most beautiful turquoise blue eyes."

"I wouldn't presume to ever criticize Danny and don't you."

"Certainly not," she exclaimed huffishly, "but she is in love with you. I've seen those freshly ironed pajamas on the chair in your dressing room. My God, there was a peaked ironed cotton handkerchief in the pocket."

"So? Danny irons napkins well, too."

She sipped appreciatively.

"So she loves you. Have you been so spoiled you don't know the difference?"

My lips moved before the words came.

"I believe you have confused love with mutual affection and respect. Danny knows this. True, that after so long I couldn't conceive of life without her, but we're together to the finish. She'll never have cause to worry. I'm leaving her this house and what money in trust for her life."

"Light me a cigarette. Mine are in my bag."

"There're Camels in the silver box on the tea table."

"Camels?" Her eyebrows rose like two crows taking off. "But you don't smoke Cam—. You have a good memory."

"For what I want. You'd be drinking Stolys rather than Absolut, which is what I drink, had the liquor store not mix-uped my order. Next time—"

"Should I read something into that?"

I liked the way her hands held the silver lighter. She placed the ashtray on the rounded arm and took a long draw.

"Read anything you like."

"Oh, you are spoiled," she chided. "Tell me, how much do you pay Danny for her devotion?"

Her casual presumptuousness produced a dull anger in me. I had the sensation of being under an X-ray.

"I have an arrangement with Danny. When she first came she used the night nursery on the third floor. Ursula wanted to die at home. Her cancer was already terminal when discovered. Danny was in a bad way, too. Her 'liquortarian' husband had walked out on her and her credit cards were maxed to the point she had to declare bankruptcy. She was sharing a basement when she was sent by the agency. The three of us bonded immediately, as you would say. She fell in love with the house, especially the carriage house. That was the one thing we'd never touched. Spiders wrapped the interior in felted cobwebs and upstairs there were hives of wild bees. They had been there longer than anyone could remember. Honey had run down between the ceiling and walls, making sticky stains. On warm days one heard them humming busily like a simmering kettle over their combs."

She removed a piece of tobacco from her lip and gave me one of her crooked smiles.

"Sounds charming."

"Only in a Charles Adams way, but there was a Stanley Steamer on blocks covered by a tarpaulin out there. I sold the car to a collector in Charlottesville, Virginia, for a lot of cash I never reported and had the place redone for Danny. She doesn't work for me only. I don't have that much money. Between patients she's a housesitter and an animal walker. She has absolutely no expenses here. We like the same food and I pay her a small amount twice a month. Other than this house, the garden, and her work she has no personal life. You see, for all his faults, she is a one-man woman. He was the first and only man ever in her life. Now, may I sweeten your drink?"

"I'm fine."

"Are you?"

Rather than answer, she reached for the silver box.

"Then I'll sweeten mine."

"Nice music. Never heard it. Who's playing?"

That damned word again. But she was grabbing at straws so I grabbed, too.

"Eddy Duchin playing *Time on My Hands and You In My Heart*."

"Who?"

"Eddy Duchin," I repeated.

"Never heard of him."

"He was Peter Duchin's father."

"He had a father?"

"Doesn't everyone?"

"I didn't mean that," she flared with wounded dignity.

"I know," I managed to smile. "You meant you didn't know he had a famous father. Well, yes, he did. No one ever stamped his personality more on the music of Gershwin, Porter and similar composers—," I stopped myself from boring her to death. "Eddy Duchin died of leukemia in nineteen fifty-one at the age of forty-two. The same age as my Father. What's playing is part of his collection of seventy-eights."

"You are lucky," she again had to remind me. Though so true, it was so uncomforting what with the sun dying like the colors in the Seraphi and the fire I was too lethargic to stoke. She put out her cigarette, stood, and finished her drink efficiently.

"I think I'll have a bath before dressing. You won't need to put in a time call. We'll use my car."

"Whatever you want," I said without rising. "We'll leave at seven. The club has valet parking."

"As I said," her resonant alto repeated, "you're lucky."

I swirled the vodka around in my glass, paused, and looked into space. "Am I?" I added rashly in a low tone as she swished out.

# Chapter Five

*Her words stopped me and burned my brain. There was a strange* roaring in my ears. I couldn't seem to make myself move. She stood at the top of the stairs demure in black and pearls and in actuality was more suited for a pinafore. Straining for something to say, I dredged out, "Ohhh that's too bad," and tried not to be overtly disappointed by her, "I'll be driving back after dinner. If I work all day Sunday, perhaps the proposal will fly on Monday. I shouldn't have come. It's all I can think about. I knew the proposal wasn't good enough when I left this morning."

To do or say something until the gap between us closed, I mentioned lightly, "If you're worried about the marital bed, the mattress is—"

She only eyed me and in an amused cynicism of her own answered, "If that were the case, I'd never be able to sleep anywhere."

I strained a smile, but I was hurting, hurting underneath everything else.

"Who are all those portraits of lining the stairs?" she inquired in a humorless fashion when I automatically reached out to take her hand.

I frowned trying to remember.

"What? Oh...Ancestors. Must you leave tonight? Why not leave early Sunday?"

She tilted her head to one side, her hair swinging.

"You'd understand if you ever let the real world in."

"There is no real world anymore," I put in dully.

"Maybe not. Not your world certainly. Why do I feel that statue is someone I know or knew?"

"Because it's Aurora posed as Diana of the Hunt."

"Shouldn't she be in a garden?"

"Not in any garden I'm familiar with. I may hang my hat on her bow, but I respect her highly. She's a reminder of all those fine bright days that won't come back. Please stay," I asked gently.

She handed me her coat as if it were a limp body.

"I can't."

"So be it."

She slipped into the waiting coat so businesslike.

"Who plays polo?"

"Nancy Mackall."

"You know Nancy Mackall?"

"I know *all* the Mackalls. Four generations of them."

That sounded pompous. I didn't care.

"Nancy gave me those mallets. It was she who placed them there. Do you know Nancy?"

"No, but I've seen her play at Brandywine. She's the best."

"So they say. I don't play. It takes six ponies," I added as I fumbled with the burglar alarm. God but I hate security systems. Bloody hell they are. Especially with her watching me.

"There, that does it." I announced with feigned indifference.

"Would you like to drive?" she inquired.

"Actually, yes," I told her, for I was thinking of Browning's *The Last Ride Together*..."Who knows but the world may end tonight...I'd hoped she would love me. Here we ride..."

She opened the door and the cold rushed in. Sharp wind carrying more than a hint of snow.

I drove with her beside me, hurting and more or less silent when we should have been laughing, teasing each other, doing small outrageous things out of high spirits. As it was...well, as it was, we were like a couple of frozen prisoners. I lowered my window and threw my cigarette out before starting over with her.

"I wanted more than to bump you in a closet on a cold dark night."

"A bump in a closet on a cold dark night," she repeated, rolling the words around.

"That's not what I meant," I flared. "I'm trying to explain why...well, why I haven't made a pass."

"What an old-fashioned word," she tweaked.

"I'm an old-fashioned man."

"We certainly can't debate that."

"No, let's have no more debating, bandying or sparring. What I feel for you is echelons above reason based on our brief encounter, and mixed up with all this is my aroused state of paternal feeling."

Her expression was ominous.

"You can scratch parental feelings to start with," she jerked. "Just what do you want?"

"I want...I want us to be sweethearts."

"God, you're incorrigible!"

"An incorrigible what?"

"An incorrigible romantic."

"So."

"So suppose I can't give you what you want?"

"What I need," I corrected and waited, steady eyes on her own.

"What is it about me that...that makes you want me? Want me enough to disturb such an ordered life?"

Then she waited, steady eyes on my own. I smiled at her, a poker player's smile.

"Your drive, while feeling no compunction to emulate. Your crooked smile. Your seemingly indestructible youth. Your apparent courage. The way you face life. And if you had dropped me off rather than waved me off in Wilmington I would have forgotten you as I've forgotten many."

The noise of the engine fell on my ear. My hands gripped the wheel. Someone almost directly in our path shouted and waved a cup. I swerved and was physically aware of her shoulder touching mine.

"Do I pass?"

Her expression turned blank. She drew her collar closer about her chin and glanced back at the man.

"I don't know," she sighed. "I really don't."

I leaned back against the seat, conscious of fatigue, of a let-down feeling. My nervousness increased her own self-possession. She staved off with, "You're an excellent driver. Cautious but confident."

"So I've been told."

"But not in a long time."

"That's true. You know, I wasn't this nervous when I went to my first dance. In fact, I wasn't nervous at all. Excited yes, but not like this. I had nothing to be nervous about. I dance very well and was born a social animal."

"Oh, I don't need convincing," she answered with a fresh, infectious laugh.

"Let me be a part of your life."

She held the flame of a match to her cigarette.

"You must be patient," she said solemnly.

"I don't want to be patient. I want to be part of your life."

The light changed to red. I braked sharply. My eyes sought her for affirmation. She closed my lips with a light kiss. The traffic blurred.

"Do you...do you love me at all?" I asked her.

I had to know and she reproved with, "How on earth do you expect me to answer that?"

"Yes or no would suffice."

I would have settled for a nod.

This time I was not to be put off.

"Then give me the odds on your loving me."

She colored as if vexed.

"I don't play odds."

She was honest. I couldn't make her seem anything else.

"And I didn't drive down just for a quick 'bump,' if that's what you thought."

Male vanity precluded my believing that. I smiled tightly.

She made a smoke ring.

"And I didn't come down just for a romp. That really isn't important to me."

I could hardly hear her.

"I came...I don't know. You intrigued me, I guess. I've never met anyone like you. Things haven't been that good between the doctor and me."

She put out her cigarette and quickly took another. I asked, "Where's the defroster?"

"There."

She stretched forward and moved something.

"Thanks."

"What about you? You and Calypso?"

I regarded the stalled M Street traffic with flat dislike. My breath caught heavy in my lungs.

"Calypso doesn't matter. No one counts but you. I'm more Calypso's guardian than lover although I am that. My wild, temple-pounding love for her wore out a long time ago." Meeting her eyes was difficult. "I only married Ursula to...to try to hurt Calypso. I was never Calypso's first love. The whole face of the world has changed since I met you." I looked to her to affirm this, waiting for it. But she said nothing. The corners of her mouth drooped like a child's and her eyes were as clear as a child's but troubled. I wanted her to look at me with shining eyes. I was conscious of my quickened pulse. The silence was broken by her voice. She whispered, "Not to worry." I savored the words and she begged off with, "Danny didn't show me the third floor nursery. What's it like?"

What lies behind us and what lies before us are tiny matters compared to what's between us now.

"Rather sweet, quaint and undisturbed. It was Aurora's as a child. There's a frieze of happy rabbits and the linoleum is patterned in toys. The only high seat in the room is the rocking horse. The chairs and tables are low and the cushions faded like the matching curtains. There's even a to-scale, roll-top desk and swivel chair. An immense fireguard covers the hearth. I keep it unchanged that way out of love."

"Yet you...and Ursula," she turned askance, "never had children."

My face darkened.

"No, we didn't. Ursula...well, Ursula," I ended, "had an unnatural fear of childbirth and pain. Thankfully, her cancer was of the liver. She never knew pain. The house became our child and the house held us together. Abetting her in this was the price I paid for not loving her."

Faced with this confession, she merely mumbled, "Enough," and touched my hand.

Yes, it was enough. More than enough. I quickly entwined my fingers in her hair and brushed her cheek with my lips before a horn sounded.

# Chapter Six

*The next morning I felt all right. That is, except for my devitalized* spirits. I felt the world was one large eternal funeral. She makes the nights too long. Bad enough that she had to wave me off in Wilmington. Last night she mother-hened me on leaving with, "Go back in the house. You're not wearing a coat. You'll catch cold. I can hear your teeth chattering."

Before bringing her things down she'd asked to see the nursery. She could have seen anything as long as she didn't leave. "Of course, you may," I smiled hard, leading the way and throwing the door wide for her. Shafts of moonglow made the day nursery a living thing. Still, I snapped on the nightlight inside the exuberant china castle atop the stencilled chest-of-draws. Lighted, its windows and turrets shined on the brown wicker framed photograph of an uncommonly sulky Aurora wearing a school uniform. Perhaps it was the restricting stiff collar and tie that made her appear so. The night was as full of Aurora as the mantlepiece, and the intruder clapped her hands with delight at the copy of the Dream King's maddest fantasy.

Rather unfairly, I motioned my guest to a low-cushioned stool and took the red-harnessed, black-dappled wooden rocking horse where my hands sought the reins out of a childish habit and sat motionless. I was dangerously near to loving her too much, and I mightn't get over it for a long time. She would get over whatever she felt by getting away tonight. I watched her clasp her hands on her knees. Her vitality, her daredeviltry, all that armor, would carry her while she was young. But it was a less durable temperament to my worshipping disposition and how calmly unconscious I was of the idiocy of a grown man riding a spotted horse that brought forth her quick impish smile. It's hard for me to conceal the thrill that I feel watching her with her hands hugging her knees on the low stool. Soon she'll be gone from me. I'm under her spell and she's leaving. It's as if my heart is broken and won't ever mend.

All I could remember of our dinner was her exquisite manners. How she waited for me to begin each course. The way she graced the table. Her perfect posture. Her appreciation of the surroundings and fine food. I strained to keep things light. Retelling stories I dine out on or pull out for interviews. And all the while I swallowed food I could not taste. In retrospect she added little or nothing to what I already knew. However, I'm congenitally incapable of asking personal questions. Yet she charmed me no end by putting a book of matches in her bag when she thought I wasn't looking and declining gold-foiled chocolates for brandy. Afterwards, at the Willard, my knowledge of the hotel's history impressed her. Over our second set of drinks in the Robin's Nest I entreated her to reconsider.

"Look, you can lock the door if you don't trust me...or yourself."

The set expression on her face was answer enough, but I went on with, "It's going on eleven. It could snow."

She came back with, "I wouldn't have to lock the door. You're a gentleman and I'm—"

"Used to walking out," I finished woodenly.

Nettled, she rebuked with, "Remember it's you who said that."

Suitably reprimanded, I signaled for the waitress who called out my name. This had caused my young companion to suddenly and jealously accuse, "Obviously, that woman knows you well."

"I've never laid eyes on her."

"She knows your name."

I stared at her trying to think why the use of my name had inspired this.

"The woman has my credit card to keep a running tab."

Her chin lifted.

"Well, she finds you attractive. I can tell."

"That may be," I cried out impatiently, "but, though she does have two-story legs, she must use an aspergill to apply her scent. Too much scent turns me off."

My gloomy reverie of all this was pierced by her laughter. "If only your readers could see you," she chided, raising an amused eyebrow. "I wish I had a camera."

I sat on undeterred.

"Let them."

"If you say so," she averred.

"I do and do you think fate had anything to do with our meeting?"

"I don't believe in fate. Why?"

"Besides Bud not showing up, why were you at your parents that afternoon and not at your office?"

"Oh, I see what you're driving at. Well, fate had nothing to do with it. I had cramps that morning. That time of the month to be blunt about it."

That certainly was. I asked for her address and phone number.

"Contact me at the office."

I stopped rocking.

"Why?"

"Because my parents would start asking questions. You may not recall them, but they know you. Father has started one of your books."

"Not you? I'm crushed."

I was.

"Which one?"

"Don't know. I'm not big on reading," she excused, "sorry."

"When we go down I'm going to give you the first half of my new book."

"What's it called?"

*Carnival of Souls.*

"Nice title, but why me?"

"So you'll get to know...understand me perhaps. Will you promise to read it?"

"I guess."

"Good. After you've finished you can decide."

"Decide what?"

"Decide if you..." I gave her a peremptory look to keep her quiet "...just read it."

She squared her shoulders and silence was her reply. I dropped the reins and stood.

ॐ

When I came to take her things down, I found her peering at her reflection at Ursula's dressing table. She turned startled, as if I'd caught her in some act.

"Danny will be hurt if you don't eat her cookies," I eased.

"I try not to eat fats. Anyway, Danny makes them for you."

"That may be, but Danny gave them to you."

"I don't have anything to wrap them in."

"Take the napkin."

"The napkin? But it's—"

"What's a napkin? Mail it back, bring it back, keep it as a souvenir with the matches..."

She flushed at that.

"...or throw it away."

Handing her the manuscript, she dropped the chapters in her grip and snapped it shut.

"Well, I guess I'm ready."

"Not quite."

I helped her with her coat, wrapped the cookies in the napkin and put them in her pocket.

"You might get hungry."

Outside the night was as cold as a vault. I took her keys and opened the trunk.

"Call me when you arrive. Call collect if you wish, but call."

"My parents and brothers always insist on my calling, too. I usually forget. Besides it will be after three when I get in."

"Don't forget and bugger the time."

"Go back inside. You're not wearing a coat. There's no need to see me off. Your teeth are chattering."

So was my heart.

"I'll wait."

Unlocking the car door, I stood back and watched her slide in.

"Do you know how to get to 495 North?" she asked looking up at me.

I couldn't believe she was driving off not knowing the way.

"No, but there's an all night—."

"Forget it. I have a map."

And with that, the car door slammed and she was off without a wave or a backward glance.

Right then I should have locked my heart to her icy frigid air. Instead, I locked the front door and waited for her call.

"Were you asleep?" she opened.

"No."

"Well, I made it back."

"I'm glad. The house seems empty without you."

"Goodnight," she clicked.

I put down the receiver filled with an empty anger.

Half-asleep and half-awake, my head was full of pictures when Danny knocked wanting to know, "Where in the hell is your guest?"

I watched the yellow line of light on the walls as Danny opened the door and heard the curtain flap and suck against the window. The old floorboards creaked as she entered bringing all the sounds and smells of my house with her. Outside, the wind was up. I heard the trees rustling.

"Her bed hasn't even been slept in. And why is your best gray suit on the floor?"

"She flew the coop as they say, Danny. Leave the suit. I'll hang it."

"Is she crazy or something?"

"Or something, Danny."

No other explanations are called for with Danny. And no reproaches either. She is a realist. She sees clearly. Sees deeply. She gave me an inscrutable look.

"Well, put on your robe and come downstairs. You look terrible. Breakfast is everything you like."

She threw me my flannel robe.

"It's for the best you know."

"Is it, Danny?"

"Yes, it is."

"Why?"

"Because it would have been like making it with a niece," she replied placidly.

"If you say so," I finished awkwardly.

"I do," she admonished. "You'd be building yourself up for an awful letdown by falling in love with her."

In that long moment that followed, I acknowledged the truth of what she said by getting out of bed and fumbling with my robe. Barefooted, I hobbled on my heel to the bureau for a pack of cigarettes. The third drawer opened and closed soundlessly. Danny handed me my lighter and I followed her as best I could downstairs to 'everything you like.' She would definitely have to have my prescription for zyloprim refilled.

'Everything I like' was flat, flat, flat. That is everything but the rich black coffee. 'Everything I like' included cheese grits, poached eggs, country fried steak, with white milk gravy, buttered hot biscuits, and French toast smothered in confectioner's sugar. Any other time my cup would have runneth over, so it must be love. I took no joy in the garden room though Danny had done the table proud. I couldn't remember when we'd breakfasted this grandly. Still, I pushed my plate away and closed my eyes, remembering. Danny sat where my guest should be. We feel no need to fill every second with conversation. It was I who ended our silence. I opened my eyes. She was waiting.

"Danny, give me some of your good advice. Tell me how to forget her and get on with my life."

"By reminding yourself that she's *just* a girl."

I grimaced.

"Surely," she added reasonably, "you weren't planning on...on running off with her?"

This was unanswerable, but my reasonable reply wasn't.

"Danny, I don't want to finish out my life without loving someone."

This fart of rhetoric caused Danny's face to go quiet and somber. Hurt flickered behind her eyes. She pinched her cigarette so tightly it wouldn't light.

"Answer me this," she asked softly, "What would the two of you ever have in common? Why, even you and that..." Danny said the name straining at her own impotence..."Calypso are more suited. Though, I'd pack up my things should you marry that one. Why a body would need an elephant hide to live with her." She paused, her lips chewed. "Look, love ain't nothing but the blues. You're better off without the both of them. Things were just fine around here 'til you met that girl. Weren't they? You'll get over her."

My unslippered feet were as cold as the coffee I swallowed. I rubbed them together.

"You didn't get over—"

Her eyes were opaque.

"I'm not you."

"And what would I do without you, Danny?"

"That's one thing you don't have to worry about. Unless.... Rain's called for this week. You better see about the roof now that you have the money."

The thought of dealing with roofers just about finished me off.

"What's your schedule like this week, Danny?"

My smile did not fool her. Or get around her.

"Why?" she sniffed.

She scanned me with shrewd eyes from across the

table. Usually she finds my smiles difficult to resist. Her face brightened and her eyes met mine.

"All right, I'll see to the roof, but only if you go in for a physical. Lord knows it's time. It's been over three years and you're headed straight for a midlife crisis."

I eyed her sharply and she returned my look with calm omniscience.

"What are you talking about?"

"Male menopause. Don't scoff. I know what I'm talking about. Daddy was about your age when he became a skirt-chaser. Then after a year or two he quieted down and lost all interest in it. I asked Mama if she missed it. Mama said, 'Not in the least, 'cause I was never interested in it in the first place.'"

I pulled the pack of cigarettes from my pocket and tackled the cellophane.

"For your information, I'm not your 'mama' or your 'daddy', Danny."

"I know," she boomed in high good humor, "so call Dr. Herrera. His office has called here twice this year trying to schedule an appointment for you."

The cigarette tasted stale. I wished I'd cleaned my teeth.

"I'll call first thing tomorrow morning. I promise."

Danny cackled with amusement.

"I'll call the roofer when you tell me what day you're going. Cheer up, turning fifty means you can stop sucking in your stomach."

"Bless your warm agreeable self, Danny. The man's card is in my black address book under 'R' for roofer."

With things settled her way, she stretched herself and stood with her back to the fire, ashtray and constant coffee mug in hand.

"I have things to tend to. I can't be sitting away the morning nursing your poor bruised ego. The silver should have been polished last Thursday, but what with getting that room ready...well, I—"

"Let me help you," I jumped in. "I won't be going to church this morning."

"You are jumpy," she accused. "You've never in your life polished a piece of silver. Now if you've really set that mind of yours on not going to church, go take a shower and call...and call Calypso. If you could only see that hangdog expression on that mug of yours. Men," she snorted.

I went upstairs, but I didn't take a shower. I disregarded heartbreak ahead to write and tear up eight dreadful letters before calling Calypso who picked up on the first ring.

"Pedophile!" she screamed.

"Have you by chance been tapping the vodka bottle you keep stashed in the downstairs commode tank? Or have you just gone plain nuts?"

"Neither and don't you dare try to deny it. You were seen."

"Seen by whom?"

"The Cushings."

"Which one?"

"Then you admit it?"

"I admit nothing, Calypso. I only asked which one."

"Why?"

"Because one is myopic and the other half deaf."

"Together they operate very well. Like Nick and Nora."

"Nick and Nora who, for Christ's sake?"

"Nick and Nora Charles. Stop trying to change the subject. The Cushings were at The National for *The Phantom of the—*"

"How many times have they seen it already?"

"Stop it!"

"Stop what? The real phantom is Andrew Lloyd Webber. All his music sounds alike. One is unable to leave a theatre humming a single—"

"You shit. They saw you in the Robin's Nest after the show. Saw you with that child and heard your name called out. You're filthy, you know that? I hate you. Locksley told me the child wasn't a day over fifteen. Did you bribe the bartender to prime her with drinks?"

"She'll be twenty-four in February. She's not a child."

"Then you admit it, you bastard."

"I only admit to taking a godchild to the club for dinner, to the Willard for a drink, and to Union Station to see her off."

"Your godchild. Since when?"

"Since she was born. Don't you remember. Her parents own that place outside Charlottesville. After her christening there was a party at Farmington. You came with...What was his name? Husband number two. Ursula and you had mistakenly bought the same dress at Garfinkel's. Polka dots."

"I...I...I can't remember. I wasn't myself then."

"It doesn't matter, Calypso. Everyone loved you anyway."

"Everyone once loved me."

"I always did and do."

"Get back to that child."

"Young woman, Calypso."

"If you say so."

"I do say so. She was here on business and, not knowing a soul, called me as her parents instructed."

"And you—"

"Took her to dinner. I saved you from a tiresome evening and allowed you to concentrate on the Junior League show. That's all."

"Is she...is she very pretty?"

"She has youth, Calypso."

"Did she ask about me?"

"Darling, it's been a long—"

"You're saying I'm forgotten."

"Not by our generation, Calypso. You were supreme. But—"

"No one compared. Did they?"

"No one compared, Calypso. No one even came close. But this generation—"

"They are referred to as the X generation."

"The what?"

"The X generation. They're replacing the baby boomers."

"Oh, what were we?"

"We were ourselves. I never once dreamed of working. I was too busy being worshipped."

"You still are."

"By whom?"

"By me."

"What about that...that young woman?"

"She's brand X."

"You're a cool liar, would you like to come over?"

"When?"

"After church?"

"I'm not going."

"Well, then, right now."

"Give me an hour."

"All right, but not a second more."

My lover's alibi worked this time.

# Chapter Seven

*"Pearl? Pearl who?"* she repeated, *sounding annoyed or* distracted.

Explaining made me feel old. What do schools teach today? I debated dialing her number for we'd had no contact since the night of her abrupt departure. But I dialed anyway, imagining in what kind of office the telephone rang out. This time, the receptionist put me through immediately, but not before I heard her whisper, "It's him, you know." However, this time I wasn't up to a grammar lesson.

"December seventh is the anniversary of Pearl Harbor. A day of infamy. The day the Japs bombed our naval base in Honolulu, Hawaii. The bombing precipitated World War II. I'm going to be in Philadelphia on that day. Can you meet me?"

I thought I detected a yawn before the, "I don't know. I'll have to call you back. Who's having a party?"

"No one, I'm coming up for a luncheon lecture at Racquet."

"On what?"

"Classical America. In particular, The Country Houses of Chestnut Hill. James Collins is the speaker."

"Never heard of him," she commented without enthusiasm.

Talking to her was like reading a telegram.

"You should have. Why not be my guest? His recent restorations include the Betsy Ross House and Independence Hall. The East and West Wings, that is."

"You would come up for that?"

I battled to keep my voice steady.

"Yes and do, but especially if I could see you."

I was consumed by wanting to see her. I had hoped she would diminish and disappear. I hadn't banked on her becoming like a bad toothache that wouldn't go away.

"Are you afraid of the future?"

Here was a woman possessed with an overabundance of purpose.

"No, only appalled by it and bad manners. Do you want to call the whole thing off? We seem to be a collision of two separate fantasies."

I craned my neck around to see if Danny had come upstairs to check on me.

"I can't make lunch, but I could meet you later."

"Where?"

"Let me call you."

"Did you get the account?"

"Which one?"

"The one you hurried back for. The one you did over the proposal for."

"No, they hated it."

"How was Thanksgiving?"

"All right. And yours?"

"I'll let you go."

"All right."

Calypso and I had managed through Thanksgiving with no harm done. Actually, she went through just fine. Calypso only has anxiety with people who may not remember. Among her own she's secure. I managed, but just barely. One ear was kept perpetually cocked for the call that never came and the other for the one that did. I had a growth on my prostate and blood in my urine. And a latex digit, followed by a sigmoidoscopy and a cystoscopy, is not a spiritual experience. When Hector Herrera phoned with the results of my physical it was the end of the false confidence of youth. I had to sit down. He scheduled the operation for the following Monday.

I didn't hear much of anything else after that. Only a crazy drum in the square beating a weird tattoo of *The Saint Louis*

*Blues.* I frowned at the din and felt thick-headed. Through the windows the sun managed to look warm. Orange leaves clung to the trees and a faint green persisted in the dying grass.

"Sorry, Hector, what did you just say?"

"I said, arrange for Calypso to accompany you Monday."

My mouth temporarily twisted.

"Calypso would only go to pieces, Hector, and, in doing so, half of Washington would have me dead and buried before my time. I'm telling no one. There'll be no sad songs for me. Not yet anyway."

"My friend, you must. You won't be able to manage on your own."

"So, it is that serious?"

"It's a rule. Nothing more. Nothing less. Neither the hospital nor I would release you to a cab driver." "And," he remonstrated, "stop that business about sad songs. The growth is more than likely benign. *Not* malignant. The tablets I prescribed are to reduce the size of the prostate. The results of the PSA are not alarming. So ask Calypso or—"

"What about my having Danny come for me? I'd tell her that morning to save her from worrying. The roofers are scheduled to arrive at eight, but I'm sure she could break away if they haven't finished. Sibley isn't that far after all. Is that all right?"

"Of course. Danny should plan on coming for you around two. I'll have my nurse call her."

"Thank you, Hector."

"You're welcome. Why didn't you tell me the new book sold?"

I stared at the tooled leather wastebasket that Ursula had surprised me with our first Christmas and tossed the envelope from my agent containing the letter from Turner Publishing, then bent to retrieve the rejection. I would need that for the accountant. "Though an ambitious and involving novel, it is outside our current publishing parameters." Christ! What did that mean? And Zodie Spain, the 'development coordinator,' had misspelled my name. How would she feel if I misspelled her name? Are 'development coordinators' replacing editors?

"Because it hasn't sold, Hector."

"But, a new roof."

"Only a patched roof and for that I had to sell more Potomac Electric shares. Thankfully, I've managed to beat the snow. And, more thankfully, my health insurance is paid up. So is the life for that matter. I'd sell the statue of Aurora before letting them lapse."

"My friend, you need never—"

"I'm aware of that, Hector, and for that, I thank you. I'm only speaking metaphorically. Oh, tell Cecilia the date for the Washington Assembly Christmas Dance is December sixteenth. You are my guests. I spoke to the fair Cecilia last month. Ah, Hector..."

I hesitated.

"Yes," he waited.

"About how long shall it be before...before I can...well, perform?"

"Perform? Oh, I see. You should be back in the saddle in ten to twelve days. Maybe sooner. I'll be monitoring you, so I'll let you know."

"That long? Calypso really will go to pieces, Hector. More than that, she'll lose her mind or go through major sexual hysteria."

"So I've heard," he chuckled. "You are very lucky."

My mouth twisted again. I got what I wanted, but am I? Lucky. Lucky. Lucky me.

"Until Monday then, my—"

"Wait," I didn't want to hang up. "How are the boys?"

"Well, thank God. Cecilia and I are blessed."

"You are," I agreed. "How many families have their own soccer team?"

"True," he agreed. "Expensive but true, and we wouldn't have one less. Goodbye my friend and for heaven's sake relax. You are in perfect health. Cholesterol, heart, blood pressure.

Calypso and you could live to be a hundred were you to give up cigarettes."

"I have no desire to live to be one hundred, Hector, and, as for Calypso, can you really imagine her at one hundred?"

"You made your point, better Calypso smoke. Anyway, all this will soon be behind you."

That may be, Hector, but I've become mentally paralyzed. And I am coming down with a case of the lay-me-down-and-die-sugar-blues. Or, to be more precise, cyclothymia, 'a bipolar disorder characterized by instability of mood.'

"I must go," Hector said. "Happy Thanksgiving."

"To you, too, Hector."

Danny was high on the ladder when I interrupted her foreman-like overseeing of the five men on the roof. Only reluctantly did she climb down. I couldn't help but notice how her jeans hugged her hips and stretched over her firm buttocks. She was an attractive sight in her dark navy blue pea coat, oversize Gypsy earrings and Ursula's green Wellingtons. Her eyes flew open wide at seeing me in a suit and tie so early in the morning.

"Mister," one of the men called out, "your woman sure is a pistol."

"I'm not his woman," Danny yelled over her shoulder without looking up. "I'm his housekeeper. And you needn't be thinking you've gotten 'round me. I'll be back. Where'd that boss of yours find you? Loitering in front of a drugstore?"

"You got that right, pretty mama," whistled the youngest and shortest of the five. "Hey, what about you and me making—"

Danny shot him a backward finger as I slammed the kitchen door on his, "Hey guys, I think I'm in love."

"Why didn't you tell me?" she cried when I'd finished telling her. "You hadn't any right to keep that from me."

"I wanted to save you any worry. Look, your hands are full as they are with that lot on the roof."

"I can handle them. I've handled worse."

Her face was becoming an unbecoming red. A small vein in her brow became a rope.

"I quit," she announced with cold determination. "Done with you...you get someone else to bring you home."

I went to her and put my arm about her. She leaned her head against my shoulder and sighed, and tears ran quietly down her cheeks. With my free hand I stroked her hair back from her forehead. I could hear her heart beating.

"Danny, please. I didn't mean to hurt you. I wanted to spare you and in doing so, I seem to have gone and ruined everything. Why, you know I couldn't get along without you. This is your home and your place is here with me. And I'm going to be all right."

Her voice wavered into normal strength and she answered me instantly, "We'll both be all right." She drew herself away, trying to smile. "You're selfish, you know that."

"Am I, Danny?"

"Yes," she acknowledged, "yes, you are, but in an endearing kind of way that makes me spoil you. Don't look so frightened. I'm...I'm not leaving. This time or ever. About the other, well nowadays things are scientifically conducted. You'll have the very best care."

I tried to pull a little grin at the corners of my mouth and she pulled my head down to hers and kissed me.

"Danny," I looked at her, "I'm sorry. You should command any man's admiration and," I added slowly, "love."

"You better go," she patted, "before that cab driver breaks through the door."

"Walk with me."

"Only to the door. That crew on the roof may walk off the job. How much are you paying them?"

"The check's on my desk. If you think it's too much, write another. They can take us to court."

Together we walked to the front hall. I put on my coat and called out, "I'm coming," to another series of loud raps. "What's the hurry? The clock shows you're five minutes early."

"Isn't this the number with the fare for Sibley Hospital?"

"Yes, driver, but I'm not having a heart attack."

"Or having a baby," added Danny.

"Then take your time, sir. I am early."

"Thank you."

"Well," Danny heaved.

"Well," I repeated. She was holding my gray mohair muffler. She shook her head.

"Men. On top of everything else, do you want to catch pneumonia. Here, let me put this 'round your neck."

That done, she began buttoning me up.

"Keep your overcoat buttoned. It's cold outside."

"You sound like that old Victor recording of Helen Kane," I kidded. "You've heard me play it a thousand times. Helen Kane, The Boop-Boop-A-Boop girl."

"Oh yeah, the one that goes, 'Button up your overcoat/ When it's cold outside/ Take good care of yourself/ You belong to me/ Boop-Boop-A-Boop.'"

"I guess I do, Danny."

"And me to you. Now go."

I opened the door.

"You are not to worry," she ordered.

I promised I wouldn't and stared at her standing in the wide vestibule before shutting the door.

When I returned shortly after three, almost pain-free but wobbly, the roofers were gone and the house once again my own. Danny carried a jeroboam from Hector Herrera's private-labeled stock. Hector was 'seventy-five percent certain that the biopsy will show the growth to be benign.' Danny came as close to fainting as she ever would on seeing me rolled out to her by an orderly. After she recovered, she wheeled me through the corridors and onto elevators with the proprietary air of ownership that proclaimed 'he's mine...stay away.' I rejoiced in the day the Lord had made and was glad in it. For the success of the operation. And for Danny.

About the only thing I remembered of the operation was head nurse, Lorna Doone, who said the way I talked reminded her of lanterns on a levee. I had asked her if she were named for the literary heroine or the cookie.

"Can't you tell? You're the author."

What a tonic she was. Here I was strapped flat on my back wearing a short-sleeved polyester smock and a clear plastic shower cap topped-off with blue chenille booties and she was flirting.

"The novel of course, Nurse Doone."

"Why?" she teased.

"Because your blue-black hair and eyes make you the very embodiment of R. D. Blackmore's bodacious and fiery heroine."

She took to that like a cat to cream, lapping the bowl clean.

"If you're up to it—" she whispered.

"Not likely, Nurse Doone. And certainly not today. I'm... well as you can see, I'm not at my best."

"No pun was intended," she blushed.

"Then none was taken, Nurse— Lorna."

"What I meant was, later would you autograph my copies of your books?"

"I will and would even if I weren't up to it. But only on the condition you will permit me to send you a copy of my new book, *Carnival of Souls,* if and when it is published."

In between all this mutual admiration Lorna Doone stuck me with a needle and tenderly asked that I start counting backwards from one hundred. I made it to ninety-two. I think.

That night Danny slept in Ursula's room on the sheets embroidered by nuns. I waited until I felt her snoring would mask any creaking floorboards before I slipped into the study, closing the door before turning on the light. Shivering and slightly ill, I grabbed the *Social Register* I was once in. I was dropped when Malcolm Forbes took it over. I like to think so he could get in. And once in, he dropped everyone not buying yearly subscriptions. Surely there couldn't be that many families of the same name with a daughter of the same name listed 'at home' living in Chestnut Hill. I had this crazy need to hear her voice. Even if it had to be muffled. Even if it broke the rule about calling her parents' house.

They weren't listed. It had now been nearly ten days since my young guest went not so gently into the night.

I shoved the tome back into its snug space on the shelf and headed for the door, then turned back for my black address book. Under 'C' for clairvoyant was Cassandra's number. She and I had encountered one another frequently during Calypso's last turbulent siege of the sugar blues. For a time, Calypso wouldn't move from the bed without her. I scribbled down the number and returned to my room. Only then did I dial. Dialed and waited. She answered with, "I've been expecting your call all evening."

"But...but you don't know who's—"

"It's you, isn't it? Calypso's playmate. Your new book will sell in March."

This was indeed an auspicious beginning.

"Cassandra, could you possibly come by—"

"For drinks tomorrow? Say about seven? I would be delighted. Your need to know the future is strong. I feel it through the phone. In your voice. Trust. Believe. Ciao."

"Don't you need my address?"

"Why, when I know you will receive a call from an attractive woman at ten tomorrow morning. Goodnight."

That distracted me enough so I could sleep after finishing my prayers. But I did wonder how much she charged.

❧

# Chapter Eight

*Cassandra is the best. The call came at ten as she said it would. That* the woman was Amanda I could not hold against her though my voice did not attempt to disguise my disappointment. Desire for Cassandra's accurate knowledge burned hot in me like a live coal.

"Should I call back on a better day or not bother you again?"

"Amanda, Amanda, you musn't be so sensitive. I'm sorry. Forgive me. It's just I'm not myself this morning."

"So what's wrong you roaming Romeo?"

"I'm recovering from prostate surgery."

"What! When?"

"Yesterday."

"Why didn't—"

"There's no need to take umbrage, Amanda. I didn't tell anyone. I'm a, well, private man. I'm only telling you now that I'm fine. Let's say no more about it."

"Then you should be dancing."

"I've also had my third rejection. This one had my name misspelled."

"Holy shit!"

"Yeah, I might as well be writing with invisible ink."

"You know you're good."

"So they said. Maybe I've passed my prime."

"Baby, you're in your prime."

"Well, at the moment, I'm blocked."

"I figured that when the pages and cajoling calls stopped. What you need to change your luck is to find a—"

"I did. Or rather she found me."

"I knew it. Screw your ranking order and move her to the number one position."

"How did you—"

"How many books have I typed? And *read?* And I mean read. I don't just type. Isn't that why you pay me so well? But after so long with you, I'd do it for free if it ever came to that. And if that doesn't cheer you up, you're in love, And good for you. Men weren't made to be monogamous."

"That's a strange comment coming from a woman."

"Coming from a realistic, honest woman who thanks you for the gladiolas Danny dropped by. Do you think I like tall flowers because I'm so tall?"

"It's possible, Amanda. Oh, did—"

"You don't have to ask. I saved you half a pan of cornbread dressing. Made just the way you like it. Lots of giblets and sage and onion and—"

"Stop, Amanda, I'm already salivating."

"What do you plan on doing when I hang up?"

I told her what she wanted to hear. Amanda doesn't know how intimidating blank paper can be.

"Go to my desk and make myself write."

"That's my man. Just sit down, start thinking and I know it's going to flow. Now, I really must run. Trying to cheer you up is making me late for a shoot, and besides you know how I hate talking on telephones. Nieman's using me for some local spots in a nine thousand dollar Bob Mackie dress of clinging gold lamé. In it I look like that actress from *Goldfinger*."

"Pussy Galore."

"Trash mouth."

"That was the character's name, Amanda. And don't let anyone spray you with gold paint."

"Why?"

"That's how Goldfinger killed Pussy."

"And season's greetings to you!"

Another woman called at twelve-thirty. That woman was Calypso. She opened with, "Why didn't you let me know?"

"Who told you?"

"Danny."

"Danny?"

"Yes."

"Danny surrendered?"

"Let's call it a truce. No white flag was extended, but her calling made me decide to forgive and forget. I've gone so far as to buy her a bottle of Shalimar."

"Shalimar?"

"And why not? It's the only scent she uses."

"I didn't know that."

"At least, that's reassuring."

"What's that supposed to mean?"

"Nothing. Why didn't you tell me?"

"I didn't think you could handle it."

"I couldn't have. When will you know?"

"Sometime tomorrow."

"Would you like me to be with you? Danny doesn't want you to be alone."

"I know. She went out and bought herself a beeper and showed me how to use her cordless phone."

"I can understand her buying a beeper, but why must one use a cordless phone?"

"It seems that beepers are not compatible with rotary phones."

"Oh."

"I have trouble though. My fingers push two buttons at the same time."

"The thing sounds horrid. I'm sorry you had another turndown. Danny told me."

"It's all right. It doesn't hurt."

"Danny said she will be gone for three days. Want to sleep over?"

"Thanks, but no."

"I'll do a hamper then. We'll lunch *al fresco*. Would you like that?"

"Very much, Calypso."

"What about a sherry chicken salad with cashews and white grapes?"

"Better leave off the sherry."

"True. Are you experiencing much discomfort?"

"Only when I whistle. Sometimes I'm forced to...Hector says the pain dissipates slowly. Calypso..."

"Yes?"

"When was the last time you had a physical?"

"After my first divorce. I thought I was pregnant, God forbid. I was absolutely riddled with guilt that a bunny had to die. I even offered to give the poor thing a Christian burial, but I was jubilant not to be with child."

"Don't you think..."

"No, I don't. I'd rather not know. Mother went through the shame of disfigurement and died...well, you know, you were there. Then there was Ursula. The dearest...the sweetest. The only woman friend I ever had. I miss her as much as Mother. Should I...well, I'd kill myself. No shilly-shallying for me."

"My God, Calypso, you'd be damned to hell forever."

"God would understand. I know He would. Do you think I'd let you or any man, much less specialists and doc—"

"Don't be insane, Calypso. That wouldn't matter to me."

"I know, but it would to me. It's my body. My aging, but beautiful body."

"Calypso—"

"I'll see you tomorrow about this time. You are sure?"

"Very sure. Thank you, Calypso."

"For what?"

"For the truce with Danny."

"The operation has changed you, darling."

"Perhaps."

For the third time since I woke to sleet and snow, I thanked God for the 'like-new roof' Danny had bullied out of the five men before paying them with the check I'd written. "Believe me, I made them earn every dime of your money," she boasted. Of that, I was certain. Now, I thanked Him again as I looked down into the bleak treacherous street. The wind blew harder.

It rattled the panes in the old windows and howled down the chimney. The fire crackled and spit out cinders against the fire screen with the ratatat of a machine gun. My house is notably empty without Danny's concerned self. She's taken on the evening as well as the day shift since the other companion quit 'the mean- faced old bitch,' while the woman was away visiting her daughter. I realize a French whore's bath doesn't suit me. I don't feel clean. Still, it's a small price to pay and I am out of pajamas and back in my regular gray flannels and navy sweater. Only today I've resurrected a tweed jacket that, too, is 'like new' since Danny sewed on suede elbow patches. I have stuffed a yellow cotton handkerchief in the pocket as an afterthought to add a cheery touch. I heard the clock strike the half hour and watched as Calypso skidded to a stop. Her red toy is splattered in filthy slush. I made my way down to unlock the door, wondering if the weather would prevent Cassandra from coming.

"Punctual for a change, I'm flattered."

"I won't let it become a habit, I can assure you."

"Of that, I'm sure. Here, give me those things."

She paused dramatically in the doorway. Calypso herself was not unlike an imperial cat. I, who have seen her beautiful without make-up, today thought her face pale. The luminous eyes had shadows underneath. There was a somber appearance about her. Even so, I saw her as I always do when she's in a room. First. One always does. The tawny hair that makes all other shades seem dead, gleamed.

"One would think we were headed for the Gold Cup, Calypso. Why the lap robe and why—?" I closed and locked the door. "Why the two long switches? Have you planned for us to indulge in self-flagelation?"

"They're for roasting marshmallows. You know very well I was never one for anything but traditional, rip-roaring sex. We're picnicing in the study. The garden room would be absolutely beastly on such a vile day. I've brought everything. Danny's domain needn't be disturbed. No woman wants another in her kitchen...or bed. You still have a lot to learn about women."

Finished with me for the moment, Calypso pulled the fur-lined canvas poncho over her head and walked to the cloak room under the stairs, sleekly feline in canary riding britches and burnished boots. The tightly-fitted jacket that flared out at the waist only accentuated her feline body.

"Has Hector called?" she asked, running her fingers through her hair.

"No, not yet," I replied, following the hips that undulated to the tick and tock of the clock up the stairs and keenly aware that a cusp of some kind would be reached between us today.

"The house looks marvelous. Danny is a treasure I've come to realize."

"A national treasure, Calypso."

"Then you realize how lucky you are."

"Of course."

She shot me a peculiar glance.

"Well, it's to your credit that you do."

Calypso should be carrying a crop. Instead, I wondered if a gun were in the hamper. For the condemned man was to be given a hearty dinner or, in my case, an *al fresco* repast before being put down.

"That Esmay of mine comes to me looking like a Fourteenth Street hooker. She refuses to wear a uniform, but I make her wash her face. Why, I don't know, for she steals my make-up like mad. It's become so bad I'm leaving her notes on what not to take when I'm running low. It's a terrible bother because I was never one who lived to shop. She also puts on my clothes when I'm not there."

I played along.

"How can you tell?"

"By that awful cheap scent she wears. I've tried giving her other scents, but she doesn't like them. When I think of Asia Minor...I don't know what I'd do without your man, Trap. Esmay calls him 'Hombre' and tries to vamp him."

"Is Trap taken with her?"

"Not in the least. The other day she asked him if he liked her 'toiltee water.' 'So that's where that stuff you're always wearing comes from,' he told her, not mincing his words. No, Trap hasn't succumbed, but the trashmen and garbage collectors have. I don't think they have any sense of smell. She tells me she was convent-schooled. 'A convent for harlots?' I said. She thought I made a 'beeg joke!'"

"Why do you keep her?"

"I feel sorry for her. She's so young to look so hard. And for all her faults, Esmay can be strangely comforting."

Calypso stopped, turned and faced me head on.

"My portraits, pictures and scrapbooks don't impress or interest her in the least, but my work does. Esmay believes in what I create. That I am a true artist. No one ever thought that, not even you. She'll sit by the hour bunched on an ottoman, biting those over-red nails that match her lips, watching me and I'm not paying her. She does it on her own time. And she won't take anything. I've tried. 'Too fine,' 'too beautiful,' she cries and backs away from what I try to give her."

"Calypso, not just Esmay admires and believes in your—"

Interrupted by the phone, I pushed back on her the things I carried to answer. Hector roared through the receiver, "Benign! Benign! You can crack open that bottle. No, you'll have to wait for that part of the celebration until you're off the medication. See you Friday at three. Nurse Doone sends her best. How do you do it, my friend? Best to you and Calypso."

"Calypso's here with me now..." Hector was gone and I couldn't move. I stood with the receiver at my ear, listening to the dial tone.

"Tell me everything," Calypso ordered, taking the receiver and hanging up.

"Benign! I'm to see him Friday. And...and I'm not to drink. Not while I'm on medication. And he sends us his best."

Nurse Doone was forgotten. Calypso and I kissed with abandonment until I became conscious of being hungry. Very hungry. Really hungry.

"Calypso," I said releasing her, "we're going to celebrate. I'm going to put on a stack of Mr. A's finest."

While not my god, Fred Astaire was everything I'd wanted to be. Fred Astaire was smooth, suave, debonaire, dapper, intelligent, witty, and wise.

"Calypso, remember this? Calypso—"

Her face was flushed with pleasure and pride at seeing her silver champagne bucket high on its stand above the highboy's middle finial.

"I won't say I'm not pleased, darling. How does Danny keep it polished?"

"By climbing up and down that ladder every other week. She maintains it's the most beautiful piece in the house."

"She does?" Calypso asked slightly unbelieving.

"Yes, she does, Calypso. Let's call her. She's waiting to know, too."

"Tell her I have a surprise for her."

I picked up the unnatural invention and fumbled three times with Danny's number.

"Let me try," Calypso offered.

"Here."

"How does it work?"

"One dials the number, waits for a beep, then dials in the area code and number one is calling from, and hangs up."

"What's the number?"

"The number's there, written on the pad."

Calypso also failed.

"The buttons are terribly close together and my nails aren't even that long anymore. I know, give me a pencil. I'll use the eraser end."

"Now what do I do?"

I repeated the instructions and Calypso finessed her way through with the use of the pencil.

"Now hang up, Calypso, and we'll wait."

We didn't wait long and I didn't give Danny time to ask.

"Benign, Danny!"

"Praise the Lord. Who told you not to worry?"

"You did, dear Danny."

"Is Calypso there?"

"Yes."

"Tell her—"

"You tell her," I laughed, handing the receiver to Calypso.

"Yes, Danny? Salley Bowles? The bitch tried to mate with a Mitsubishi and the thing ran over her. When? Over a year ago. Yes, it was traumatic, but to think a bitch of *mine* would have indulged in miscegenation is appalling. You're darling to have asked about her. Lemon squares? You didn't! Why, they're my favorite. We'll have two desserts. The other? We're going to roast marshmallows. Well, yes, of course, we'll be careful. Oh, I hope you'll like my small surprise. Goodbye."

"Be careful of what, Calypso?"

"Be careful of the andirons and don't use the poker for roasting the marshmallows. I felt like a child again."

"Danny does have that effect at times," I agreed.

"And a small price to pay for such a treasure. Let me give you her present before I forget. It's in the hamper."

What Calypso handed me resembled a Faberge egg.

"Why it would be criminal to open this, Calypso," I complimented truthfully.

"Thank you. Damn! I've smoked my last cigarette."

"I have plenty Calypso. Danny put in two cartons yesterday. They're in my room."

"Don't bother, Ursula always kept your father's silver box full. Doesn't Dann—"

Calypso's memory for what was once, nailed me.

"You don't smoke Camels. Neither do I...perhaps they belong to a ghost upstairs. Or, have you gone and changed partners on me?"

Fred was singing to Ginger, *Let's Face the Music and Dance.*

"Calypso..."

"I think we can do without Fred, don't you?"

On that note, Calypso and I might as well have picniced in the sleet such was the cold war that existed between us.

"Want to finish this?" she asked complacent-voiced.

I shook my head. Calypso splashed out the last of the Bloody Shame. Red ran to the rim of the glass. She licked her fingers, then drew hard on her cigarette, made a face, and threw it into the fire with her caution.

"Did I tell you Nesta rang?" she smiled coolly, turning over and drawing up her knees.

My lips tightened. I stabbed the pearl-handled fruit knife into the pear I was peeling and wiped my mouth with a napkin.

"When?"

"Just after my call to you yesterday."

"You didn't mention my—"

"Of course not, darling."

"Thank you."

"She wished us a belated Thanksgiving. I told her about ours in Warrenton with the Derbys."

"Nesta's a brick."

Calypso couldn't wait to pounce.

"You failed to tell me that the train you put your 'godchild' on was the train to Philadelphia."

"So."

I refused to nibble at her bait.

"So, I know all about Bud, and 'lovely child.'"

"Who?"

"The 'young woman' who drove you to the 30th Street Station. Don't play the innocent with me. You've become quite untrustworthy."

I stubbed out another half-smoked cigarette.

"No more than you."

Calypso moistened her lips.

"True, but I've never taken advantage of a person's confused mental state."

"No, you only caused my mental state as well as causing your own."

"That is not the point. You used my belief that all babies and sailors look alike against me. Also the fact that my second husband remains a fuzzy blur except for the fact that his outlandish ties always made me think he had to be colorblind."

"As I recall, your memory lapses ended when signing...his name was Palmer...when signing Palmer's name to checks. But to get back to what you think happened, Calypso. Nothing happened. The wolf in me was not smart. He left me my heart."

"Then you were a fool. Nesta says there's been talk...rumblings really. Nothing definite, but—"

"Calypso," I warned jerkily, "if you told Nesta anything I'll—"

"Of course not, pet, discretion being my middle name, but I did listen to what Nesta had to say and there is talk of an older man..."

I was turning red.

"...not you, I mean really old...sixty-six or seventy plus...who lives in Chestnut Hill but keeps a pout house, well, actually, a place for assignation, in center city. He's either an attorney or doctor. I forget, but he's a man, who Nesta says, is decidedly *non-U* and makes a dangerous enemy."

"None of this is your business, Calypso."

"Darling, I am, or was, your business. You once begrudged others."

"I still do, Calypso."

She smiled. She'd caught lots of men with that smile. A vividness returned and burned with the inner flame that had been hers in the glory years.

"You think I'm resentful because of my approaching maturity. I'm not. I know you just as you know me. We've spent our lives blowing hot, blowing cold and it didn't matter to me or to you. This is fine except for our fatal weakness of occasionally putting all of our eggs in one basket. Just as you did with me—"

"And just as you did with Eddie."

"Yes, and look what it got both of us. And you would be

doing it all over again by falling in love with this girl. I'm sorry you didn't sleep with her."

"And why?"

Calypso removed one of the earrings set in rims of jade, tugged at her lobe, and reclipped it.

"We suffer chronic growing pains. We think every falling in love is the enduring thing. Wonderful, if it happens once and remains always. But that's rare and not for us. At our age we shouldn't be frittering around like that. You had it coming. Try to forget it."

Her eyes shut the way they used to just before a dive or some jump of which she was afraid.

"Love divided in two won't do and you run the risk of my not taking you back."

She took my hand and held it against her cheek. "I'm afraid," she smiled wanly. "I've always trusted you. Can't you...? Esmay refers to me as the crazy old lady. I've heard her."

Before I could reply Calypso broke away, walked to the window, and stood with her back to me. I cleared my throat and went to her, pulling her around.

"I'll never leave you, Calypso, as long as you want me and I'll look after you as long as you need me."

"I need it dreadfully. I don't see how I could get on without you."

Color came up in her cheeks.

"Don't leave me. I won't hurry you for all I have left is pride."

I held Calypso's face in my hands, stroking her temples gently with my thumbs. Her eyes were closed. She nuzzled her head in my hands. I stared over her head to the photograph taken the year she came out and said farewell to my youth.

"Calypso?"

"Yes?"

"Look out the window. One of these days," I announced firmly, "we'll go across the square to that church and get married. It may not be Berkley Square, but I'm certain nightingales will sing."

And that said, I kissed her softly, unsure of her response. Her arms encircled my waist and I increased the pressure of my mouth. Her tongue urgently curled around mine and then she drew away.

"Thank you. There'll be no further discussion of the incident, however, obscurely. I promise."

Yes, I thought, but it will always be there, between us, like a knife in the bed.

# Chapter Nine

*The dull sound of the knocker resounded through my still house.*
I rose from the twilight of sleep and hurried down the stairs
shouting, "Coming," to another series of hammered sounds. I
felt drugged out. Everything felt fifty already. I wanted a drink
and even considered rinsing my mouth with vodka as I opened
the door.

"Sorry, Cassandra. I didn't hear you pull up. I must have
been sleeping more sound—"

"I didn't come by automobile."

"Then how did—"

"Aren't you going to turn on the lights?" she inquired
curiously in a full dramatic alto.

God, so well do I know my house that I don't need lights.

"Of course, Cassandra, come in. I hadn't noticed they
weren't on."

The tall broad-shouldered woman who swept across my
vestibule cut a wide swath in her black cape and paisley shawls.
Cassandra is a personage of a kind one would have passed an
evening with in the heyday of the Orient Express. She brings
with her the air of a prima donna armored in jewels, but without
the exaggerated ego. Those Rasputin-like eyes of hers absorbed
all as she pirouetted to a halt under the branched gasolier and
remarked, "One forgets gas-lighting has been with us for a long
time."

"Actually, since the eighteen twenties," I blandly
acknowledged to the upturned face studying the burning jets of
images casting ghostly shadows on the high ceiling and surfaces

of wall that are broken by the terra cotta cornice and picture rail.

"There is a feeling of serenity, calmness and order here," she announced. "It surrounds me. I feel it."

I could add nothing to that. She regarded me and stepped forward, asking, "May I?"

"Of course, Cassandra." I smiled with good-host-graciousness, but all the time hoping that Cassandra didn't charge by the hour.

She slid back the pocket doors that in the winter are kept closed at night, and I pushed in the mother-of-pearl button.

"Yes, yes, yes," she repeated as she went through the rooms with me lighting the way. "It all flows together like an exquisite string of pearls. Everywhere one looks one sees beauty. It's as I knew it would be."

"What is, Cassandra?"

"Your space," she intoned.

"My space?"

I was slow to understand. I was thinking about abundance and desire.

"Yes, your space matches your persona, but you must take care not to become wombitized. It would be so easy for you to give in to that streak of reclusiveness that is inherent to you and your family. Three great-uncles ended their lives in reclusion. Am I not correct? And then there was—"

I tried not to appear annoyed.

"Calypso had no business telling you anything about my—"

"Calypso has told me nothing. Which brings me to Calypso. Her car is here, but she isn't. She hasn't…hasn't had a relapse? Has she?"

"Hmm, no, Cassandra. Calypso's fine, but I didn't want her driving home in this weather. At best, she's an erratic driver."

"Calypso is about to go through a transition. She will leave behind the more temporal aspects of what has been her life."

"If you say so, Cassandra. However, the temporal aspects of her life are her life. Perhaps you'd like to see the upstairs study," I said, turning off the lights. I was anxious to begin.

"Of course," she again intoned.

Cassandra made her way 'round the study slowly before sitting down on the edge of the window seat and opening her bag. I stopped banking the fire to hold the silver lighter to her cigarette. She smiled her thanks, inhaled deeply and exhaled through flaring nostrils.

"Your world is a tight little island," she rightly observed.

I noted that she wore no rings. Only a collection of bracelets on her right arm. I counted six. Two were plain gold.

She looked at me from beneath her lashes waiting for my reaction.

"I like it that way," I agreed, fidgeting with the lighter.

"I know you do," she went on, "but are you aware that the soul of this house and the center of your soul is this room?"

I let a silence fall and stopped fussing with the lighter.

"Perhaps not consciously, Cassandra, but, yes, I've somehow always known that my strength and equanimity are derived from this house and this room. I believe a house gives back ten-fold when loved. And this house is loved, Cassandra. Loved by me. Loved by Danny, my housekeeper. She felt its enchantment even before she decided to stay forever."

"Calypso has told me much of your wonderful Danny. She is…a force in your life. Is she not?"

"Danny is that, Cassandra, and more. If she were here I'd introduce you."

"Another time."

She rose, stretched out both hands, and put out her cigarette.

"The piece atop the highboy is from Calypso. I recognize her work."

I didn't want to talk about Calypso. I looked hard into Cassandra's eyes, giving a silent warning.

"There will always be something between you and Calypso. Something sheer as gossamer, strong as iron. Something that will not be dismissed or shoved aside."

Cassandra believed what she said. I could tell by the expression of her eyes. I grunted and stared out into the dark

December night half expecting to see something. Abruptly I asked what she wanted to drink.

"Do you have the makings of a scotch mist?"

I did, and she began to emerge from her cocoon of shawls and cape with my help.

"Cassandra is an unusual name for a prophetess considering what befell her," I commented once we were settled.

She turned her glass slowly and rubbed the ashes from the glowing end of another cigarette into the ashtray as they formed, turning the cigarette in her fingers.

"So you are familiar with Greek mythology. I'm impressed."

"Not really, Cassandra, but I have read Edith Hamilton's work and it was Apollo who loved Cassandra and who gave her the power to foretell the future. When she refused his love he turned against her. What she predicted was true, but no one ever believed or listened to her. Didn't she tell the Trojans six times what would befall them?"

She looked at me and said nothing, but she was disturbed by what I had said and I hadn't meant for her to be. She put her drink down without taking another sip, and I felt the need to apologize.

"Please don't think I was in anyway being cynical of your power, Cassandra. I wasn't. Being sarcastic is not my nature."

"No," she said very decidedly, "no, it isn't. But as to my name, I feel I was prophetically christened, for you will refuse to believe or listen to what I'm going to tell you. Like so many, you want me to reaffirm what you want to believe. What you should want is for me to exorcize you."

My glass of tonic water went back to the damp spot on the napkin. I struggled not to admit the truth and too sharply confessed, "My soul feels torn to shreds, Cassandra."

She nodded understandingly.

"It will never work between you and this younger woman you've met with the dark hair and stubby fingers."

I drew a surprised breath. Cassandra was making me a true believer. I bit my mouth to find out if it were as numb as it felt.

'Dark hair' could have been a lucky shot in the dark, but not the 'stubby fingers.' As if for the first time I found myself noticing the color of the partially drawn silk damask curtains. Ursula had referred to the color as...as what? I frowned with concentration trying to remember her words. Her voice. And when I did I shouted out, "Federal Blue."

"Federal Blue!" Cassandra was dumbfounded. Stunned to silence, her eyes flew wide. She reached for her drink. I tried to smile it off and failed.

"That's the color of the curtains, Cassandra. I couldn't recall what color Ursula had said they were. I don't know why it suddenly became so important. Sorry, but the person you described does have dark hair and stubby fingers. Her...her hands are the hands of a child."

"You must forget those hands. Forget her and stop being a foolish man. Must you be told six times, too? As a successful writer you should recognize that it is only the lack of certainty about her that has created this sudden passion. You're poles apart and not only in backgrounds. This girl will never understand the sense of nuance in your life. Beyond that first mutual attraction there is nothing. Will be nothing. Yes, she will take but she'll never give. Tell me, did she value being here?"

I straightened up abruptly.

"How did you know she'd been—?"

"I know. So tell me, did she feel the beauty that envelopes one?"

"She asked me if I were afraid of letting the real world in."

"And you? What did you say to such rudeness?"

"I told her there was no real world anymore."

"Then why do you refuse to believe what I tell you?"

"She's just a child," I dogmatically defended.

"She's older than you. And the truth you need is that you're too young for her. For it to work would require gene therapy and for what. You'd be throwing away happiness for something that would never make you happy. She'd never live in this house with you. With Danny. Your ways would be foreign to her. She'd be resentful of something she couldn't understand. You love this house. Your strength, your creativity comes to you from these walls. This house would reject her. She herself realizes this."

I wanted to refute what she was telling me. My chin went up but my body seemed to slump.

"If you could only meet her. Meet her once and you would—"

"I have no wish to ever encounter such a disruptive influence. You musn't waste your energy on her. Do it and it will add up to a big nothing. To put it as simply as possible, the two of you have different frames of reference. She's shifting and you're not. I don't need to ask how your new book is progressing, do I?"

No, she didn't.

"Then acknowledge that you cannot function without continuity in your life and that the relationship would be catastrophic for someone bred to optimism."

"I'll try," I ceded.

"You won't. Not right away, at least. But enough of her. Let's move on to your unsold book."

"You told me the book would sell in March, Cassandra," I reminded her.

Again she drew hard on her cigarette.

"That was true then. However, I now perceive something blocking its sale."

Her codicil finished me. I felt depleted.

"What do you mean?" I asked, almost in a state of unconsciousness resembling deep sleep. Danny's spiced pecans and brandy snaps lost their appeal.

"What I said doesn't matter. What the block is I can't see, but it's there. On the periphery. So close. Yet it escapes my understanding and grasp."

I refrained from saying, well, isn't that just peachy keen. Instead I monotonically inquired if this sort of thing often happened. An awkward moment followed.

"Very seldom," she apologized. "I'm sorry. These things can't be rushed."

"Yes," I admitted. "It must be like writing."

"Be patient."

"Patience is not one of my strong points, Cassandra."

"Of that I'm very much aware," she mollified in her most assuasive velvet voice, "still it is one you should perhaps develop. But, you're tired. You and Calypso have been at it."

I sighed heavily, "Yes, we have, Cassandra."

"It will pass."

Heading for my desk, I asked with a weary, hesitating cadence, "May I give you a check?"

"There will be no charge. You are a very charming man. You may give me a first edition of *Carnival of Souls* when it is published."

"If it—"

That she knew the title of my unsold book was frightening.

She watched me with a smile.

"No if's. Things will work out. This, I promise you."

Hours later, I stood at my desk directly in front of the telephone with my hands deep in the pockets of my flannel robe, noticing how my tools of the trade laid on the polished leather of the desk top in regimented parallel rows. I couldn't sleep and it was far too early to be up for anything or anyone. What Cassandra hadn't understood, what I hadn't told her as she left, was I wanted things to work out my way. I reached for the receiver and stopped in mid-air. I would have to wait until the office in Philadelphia opened to find out if she were planning to meet me on Tuesday. To contain myself I picked up the transition paragraph needed to connect two chapters. I hadn't looked at it since she'd so abruptly driven off. Sitting down I turned on the desk lamp and started a cigarette. Soon I was at it and if it weren't full throttle it was at least a steady, pleasing pace. I accomplished what was needed with one sentence and kept on going not bothered by the cold or lack of Danny's strong black coffee. I almost decided not to call so pleased was I with the way things were going. My finger on the hook went down. Then up. I dialed and *she* answered.

"Oh, it's you."

"Where's your charming receptionist?"

"You scared her off."

"I doubt that."

"But you did. It was pedantic of you to correct her."

"Someone had to. She's probably cost you untold accounts."

"My clients wouldn't know the difference."

"I would say that's rather a pity."

"I'm sure you would."

She did not keep the huffiness out of her voice and I didn't keep it out of mine.

"Look, I'm calling because I need to make reservations. Are you or aren't you coming? You never called me back."

"I don't think so."

"One would think I was inviting you to stand in line with me for food stamps."

"Well, can you meet me at three for drinks?"

"Where?"

"The Ritz-Carlton."

"There's one in Philadelphia?"

"Yes, in fact there's a whole unexplored world outside of clubdom."

I know. That's why I belong to clubs.

"Where is it? Never mind, I'll be there."

"So will I. Goodbye."

On that euphoric note I resumed writing. It was during a late breakfast of stale honey sandwiches that my mind made the obvious jump to Calypso. I polished off Danny's sandwiches with another glass of milk and hurried back upstairs to dial her number. It rang busy. I counted to fifty and dialed again, dialing rapidly, impatient at its slowly clicking return.

"What a surprise! Are you all right?"

"Fine. And you?"

"Better."

"Why don't I drop off your car? Say in two hours?"

"Why the hurry?"

"No hurry on my part, Calypso. I thought we might have lunch. The streets don't appear treacherous. We could walk to the club, Martin's, or what about The Tombs."

"Certainly not The Tombs. All those healthy, bright-faced Georgetown students would make me want to commit hari-kari."

"I don't know why. None of them will ever have what you had *and* have."

"Perhaps."

"Well, then, what about Martin's? All those tired old faces should make you feel positively girlish."

"Why don't we forego lunch and spend the afternoon in bed?"

"I can't. Not at least until December seventh."

"Damn!"

"Damn is right. I've started having very wicked dreams."

"About whom?"

"Need you ask? And speaking of the seventh, come with me to Philadelphia. Racquet is having another lecture luncheon on Classical America. This one is on—"

"You can't go to Philadelphia on the seventh."

"Why?"

"Because we're going to the pre-opening of the League's Christmas show at the Madison."

"Can't we do both?"

"No, we can't. I'm scheduled for an all day with Derek and I'm nervous enough as it is."

"About what? Your designs will be the hit of the show. I predict a twenty-four hour sellout. Why, I wouldn't be surprised if Bergdorf's didn't pick you up and make you another...What's her name? You have a collection of her evening bags."

"Judith Leiber. But, that's not what I'm nervous about. I'm worried about cocktails. Cocktails *prolongé*."

"I'll be with you, Calypso."

"Not if you go to Philadelphia."

"I can take an earlier train back and meet you there. It's not black tie."

"You'll meet me here! I don't *loiter* in hotel lobbies. And plan on sleeping over. We can cuddle if nothing else. Will you?"

"That's too tempting an offer to refuse. I accept."

"Whom shall you take?"

"Take where, Calypso?"

"To the lecture. What's wrong with you?"

"I'll ring Nesta."

"Nesta?"

"Yes, Nesta. She *does* live in Chestnut Hill and that *is* the subject of the lecture. What about our lunch? Are we on?"

"I think not. I need to lose five...seven pounds, really, by next week. You keep the car. Bring it by Sunday and I'll go to church with you and let you take me to The Tombs. Oh, just this morning I read this. I quote, 'The younger one's date, the older one looks.'"

"Calypso—"

"Darling, I read it in *W*. Should I save it for you? It's from a list of maxims. Another is 'Older men look better dressed than undressed.'"

"Goodbye, Calypso."

"Goodbye."

That I hadn't fooled Calypso didn't for a moment bother me, but I did invite Nesta, who accepted. I stopped my conscience by believing I'd lived all my life waiting for this young girl. Everything is the same as the day I left for Nesta's last month except me. I'm not the same. I would concern myself with Danny when the time came. When I did, her eyes met mine with electric force. She began to make a face, stopped and marched down the hall to stand against the door as if to block my passage.

"Are you crazy or something?" she asked with quick impassiveness.

My answer was a quiet one.

"Or something, Danny" and further supplied that I felt only half alive and was being driven mad.

Danny laid her hand on my arm, "Bad mud makes a bad foundation."

Air ripped into my lungs.

"What?"

"The girl never returned the napkin."

"What napkin?"

"The napkin she wrapped my sugar cookies in and took with her."

"Danny, I wrapped your cookies in the napkin. I gave them to her."

"But not the napkin which has yet to be returned."

My muscles began an agonized tensing.

"What's one napkin?"

Danny frowned. Her air and tone seemed really puzzled by my uncharacteristic indifference.

"An uneven set. And a set that belonged to—"

For a long time I did not speak.

"I don't care if the set belonged to Catherine the Great. If it will make you happy throw away another to make things even."

"Half of what's hurting you is vanity."

I stared at her, amazed and wounded.

"Vanity!"

"Yes, vanity. The younger woman taken with the older man. Well, she's not. The play's over. It closed the first night."

I had no temper, only a terrible weariness. Danny stepped aside as if to say, 'You can leave' and that there was no need for a second order. I opened the door. "Danny, I—." She spoke with impersonal, cut-off coolness, "You'll get no sympathy from me this time. So don't come moping 'round asking for any. I repeat, bad mud makes a bad foundation. My proof of that is the napkin."

❧

# Chapter Ten

*Intentionally or not, she was late. Twice I declined ordering. I'd* arrived ten minutes early. She was already twenty-five minutes late, and I asked the waiter to stop replacing the ashtrays. Let the evidence of her lateness accumulate. Though the Ritz-Carlton exterior evokes London at its worst, the bar manages to evoke London at its best. Bleached wood walls and rumpled sofas and chairs. Everything was like an expensive old shoe, getting slowly better and better. I twitched at how I'd signaled for a taxi going the other way and jumped across traffic, the lecture and Nesta forgotten, and how I'd waited for the hotel elevator with ill-concealed impatience. How hurriedly I'd stepped in and pushed the door close button before pushing for mezzanine. My depression was now unmistakable.

Edgerton Edgerton, sipping tea, observed her entrance. He, who has opened every Assembly since before the Liberty Bell cracked, raised his eyebrow just slightly before letting it fall. His lids came to half-mast behind his half-moon spectacles and he aborted his hand from tweaking his moustache. She removed one of those Edwardian-style hats of black velour that catches the light in its folds, and tossed her hair slightly to annoy him, turning left before reaching his table. Stiffly rising, I came close to her. Our eyes locked, and I felt a rush of intimate awareness between us that produced a prickling, stinging sensation in my groin. It was criminal the way she'd stolen my heart. Like taking candy from a baby. Hard and bright, I would freely let her take the reins and turn time off. I took her preemptorily by the arm. The sadness will begin when I leave her.

"How's Caroline?" she asked, slightly breathless.

"Caroline?" What about me? What about Danny?

She licked at her mouth.

"Caroline, at The Tune-Inn. Has she asked about me?"

That Caroline hadn't, I didn't tell her.

"Several times," I lied. "She's been wanting to know when I'll be bringing you back."

My bold-face lying created that false sense of past we needed. She looked at the tray full of cigarettes and the picked over bowl of nuts. A quiet seemed to settle in following the flurry on her arrival and our ordering. We both were suddenly shy. I lighted a cigarette and smiled at her. She spoke first.

"Do you approve of our meeting place?"

"Very much."

"I thought you would. It's like you."

"In what way?"

"In what you like and believe in."

"Which is?"

"Repair and restore."

"Is that so unusual?"

"To some."

"What about you?"

"Me? I replace. I throw out."

"You're still very—"

"I stayed here once."

"With whom? Sorry. Don't tease me. I won't wear a fool's cap for you or anyone."

She laughed at me.

"I met you at exactly the wrong time."

"When would have been the right time?"

"Any other time, I guess."

My shiny new balloon guesses!

"You know I love you. I love you surely and deeply and whenever I will think of you, I will love you."

She spoke quickly.

"You're moving too fast."

"I don't think so."

The room was becoming crowded. An overdressed woman

asked to borrow our extra chair for her mink. I wanted to say can't you check your coat the same as everyone else. Instead, I put the present I was saving for later on the floor.

"This may be our moment. One of those great history-making moments."

She produced a cool, "I'm afraid I'm not history-making stuff."

With an overpowering necessity to have something be funny when nothing could be, I wondered if she sometimes had trouble deciding whether she wanted to be Wonder Woman or Gigi.

"You're still a lovely creature. It's exciting seeing you again."

"When did we meet?"

"The first time was November the tenth. It was a Wednesday. The second time was November the twentieth. It was a Saturday. Why do you ask?"

"No particular reason. Just checking to see if you remembered."

"I remember."

"Does Danny polish your shoes?"

"How do you know I don't?"

"I know."

This is not the spunk I admire. Why all these uncooperative signals? I want endearments. Affection. Affirmation.

"Danny...or I take my shoes to a bootblack on the Hill, near the Marine Corps Barracks."

Across her face went an expression that might have been one of rather malicious triumph. The exuberance of seeing her was fading.

"Shineologist is the P.C. word," she amended.

The waiter silently put down his tray and backed away. I finished my cigarette and reached for my napkin.

"For me, P.C. means only perfectly comfortable and I'm perfectly comfortable with the term bootblack. So is he who does my shoes. Tell me, did you like my house?"

She broke one of the crustless watercress sandwiches

in halves. I moved my drink off the tray and to my lips, remembering, and then not caring, that I wasn't supposed to be drinking. Outwardly, she was a Sachertorte, but inwardly she was a Sacher*tart*.

"Well, I did have to push things out of my way to put something down." She paused and swallowed. "But your house doesn't look cluttered."

It's easy to keep a stiff upper lip in a soft low-back chair.

"Perhaps you carry the truth too far. Tact can—"

"It was you who asked," she justified. "Oh, I meant to bring the napkin you used to wrap the cookies. I found it under the seat the other day. I'd dropped my lipstick. I thought maybe I should wash it first."

"You can throw it away for all I care."

"Danny wouldn't like that."

"The napkin belongs to me, dammit."

"Not really. And I wouldn't say that to Danny. She believes you and the house belong to her."

"I like it like that."

"I know you do."

To wrench herself free of these truths, she sped to the question of my braces. I was wearing black braces embroidered with pink elephants and my best gray pinstripe suit.

"Are you in your own subtle way making a political statement?"

"I don't make political statements. I am what I am. The braces were a present. An English present from...from a titled English lady. Lady Judith Bateman Briggs. She presented them to me a long time ago. But I am a Republican."

"Was she really—?

"Yes, she really was, and by birth, not marriage. She works or worked for the Egg Association of Great Britain."

"Doing what?"

"Trying to convince the Common Market to buy British eggs. I have a photograph of Judith somewhere posed with thousands of eggs. I'll dig it out if you personally return the napkin."

"Would you like that?"

"How many ways must I tell you that I love you?"

She made a slightly guilty face before putting aside her drink and opening her bag. She pulled out a crumpled pack of Camels. I leaned forward to light her cigarette.

"Look at me, I'm not interested in a shoddy back street affair, just as I'm not interested in marginal sex. I'm very proud of you. I want my friends to become our friends, and I would hope the same with you. There's a dance in January that I —"

"There's not one in December?"

"Three, but I'm committed."

"To...to whom?"

"To Calypso."

"To Calypso?"

She pulled away.

"Don't be that way. Neither of us were living vestal lives before finding one another."

"What would your friends think of a mongrel?"

"A mongrel?"

"A Hoosier, then?"

"A Hoosier?"

"A Hoosier is what people from Indiana are called."

"You weren't born in Philadelphia?"

"One may be born in Philadelphia without ever presuming to call one's self a 'Philadelphian.' Didn't any of Mrs. Parry's friends tell you that my parents came from Indiana? Neither had a heritage. What they have, my Father made here."

"What does that have to do with us? With anything?"

"Old Philadelphia imposes nullity on the witness of reason. I'm sure old Washington does, too."

I shifted the position of my chair's brass casters to get away from cigar smoke coming from the fat-necked man seated at the bar.

"So you're not in the sire and dam Form Book. So what. You bear that look of race, that faint evanescent but unmistakable stamp of what was once termed quality. Is that what you really think of me?"

"You are what you are. That's what you said earlier. You can't deny it."

"I don't, but what you said has nothing to do with us, and about your parents— Who's the jock trying to get your attention?"

"Beaver Harris."

That she regarded him without pleasure didn't matter. I raged inside.

"You know someone named Beaver Harris?"

She gave him a weak smile.

"I know someone named you."

"I don't wear correspondent shoes in December!"

"Are you this possessive of Calypso?"

I chewed on my lower lip.

"I used to be."

"At least you're honest, but don't concern yourself with that boy."

"Did you know him well?"

"He only tried to rape me once. Without success," she added with her funny little smile. "But, what, tell me, are correspondent shoes?"

"Black and white saddles. At one time, according to Nesta, they were always the type of shoes worn by the correspondent in a divorce."

"I've never heard that. Do you own a pair?"

"Ummh, yes, but I only wear mine from Memorial Day to Labor Day."

"Is that a law written in stone or the length of your particular mating season?"

"Let's just say it's an unwritten law among—"

I picked up the plain manila envelope and handed it to her.

"Perhaps this will stimulate a wanderlust in you."

"What is it?"

"A small, thin unessential luxury I stumbled upon in Rizzoli's."

She dabbed at her lips. "I've never seen ribbon like this before."

"It's very old. From a wheel in the attic."

"Carefully, she slid the ribbon from the wrapping.

"The wrapping paper must be old, too. Is it?"

"Yes. It's French wallpaper."

Cautiously, she removed the paper.

"*The Pleasure of Romantic Travel*! I believe you must be a disappointed romantic!"

"Must I be disappointed? The book is not inscribed for obvious reasons and those reasons being *yours*."

She let that pass.

"I'd hoped that you'd like it."

"I do. This is my first Christmas present."

"I wanted it to be."

"I'm sorry I was late. My parents are just back from London. I picked them up this morning and drove them to our farm in Chester. Then their car wouldn't start so I gave Mother my car and drove the truck back to meet you because Mother can't or won't drive the truck."

"You're forgiven. I forgave you before you explained. Have you started my manuscript?"

"Only just. As I told you, I'm not big on reading. How long do we have?"

"Not long, I'm afraid."

"Oh."

"I'm sorry, but you only committed for drinks and I'm... I'm committed...I promised...Calypso needs me. Tonight is very important to her."

She moved her head indignantly.

"Why?"

My response was guarded.

"It's complicated."

"I see. And me?"

"I would praise God if you needed me, but I don't think you'll ever need anyone. I'm taking the four-fifty-seven back."

"Then we'd better be going."

"Yes."

I motioned for the waiter. I felt dull and very tired. She handed him a fifty dollar bill, silencing me with, "I never properly thanked you for that excellent dinner...and lunch."

We didn't wait for the elevator. We walked down.

The runner cushioned our steps. She laughed, "I think the waiter thought I was your daughter."

"I hope not, for I don't feel fatherly."

"The weather's turned miserable," she observed vaguely.

It had, and the Salvation Army soldiers didn't appear to be soldiers of Christ. For all their ringing, they might have stolen the kettle and stand.

"Where are you parked?" I asked her.

"I'm not driving *you* anywhere in a truck," she let me know. "I'll get us a taxi." And I gaped at the dark-haired girl with the slender neck and shining eyes, thinking I was the luckiest man in the world. And, anxious as I was about Calypso, feeling responsible and uneasy, stabbing through everything was the fact that I was in love. All my fine words failed me. I reached out and tugged at the loose-hanging threads on her coat. She was unselfconsciously *prachtig* in a Tyrolean suede jacket and a sensual wool challis full-sweep skirt of flame flowers on midnight black that made things happen even standing still.

"You've lost one of your buttons."

"I know," she said tonelessly, "I lost it a long time ago."

"I do love you," I told her again.

## Chapter Eleven

*Calypso's room collects all the shadows of night, evoking the* strongest memories of my loving her. Wanting her. Her soft breathing told me she had fallen asleep. Her hand moved against my chest. She pushed her hair back from her face. My chest constricted painfully. I kissed her with a kind of love and with infinite regret. We'd gone to bed, seeming to have floated free, without effort or purpose.

About Philadelphia she only cracked, "How are things in the 'City of Brotherly Love?'"

"The weather was miserable, the lunch excellent and the lecture first rate. Nesta—"

She interrupted with, "Let's not close all the doors yet, shall we?"

"No, let's not, Calypso."

Had my guilt shown all over me like a tatoo?

The train out of Boston had been delayed, and I'd just missed the Metroliner. I breathed out white smoke while waiting for Calypso to open the door. When at last the door opened it was Esmay greeting me in a tight red dress of some sleazy-looking stretch material that managed to show her hard little nipples, navel and *mons veneris* in perfect bas relief before ending high above run-down-at-the-heels white plastic boots.

"Season's greetings, Esmay," I smiled, handing her my coat. "You're working unusually late, aren't you?"

"Tonk you, senor," she giggled with a flirtatious wiggle. "Madame very excited. You late. She late. I late. Me go beeg party."

"Like that! You'll catch your death, child."

"I good girl, senor. I carry condoms."

She flashed three condoms from her cleavage wrapped in the colors of Christmas. I've outlived my time, I realized.

"Esmay, Esmay, I meant a cold. You know. Influenza. Consumption. Pneumonia."

"You make beeg joke with Esmay, right?"

"Wrong," Calypso announced from the landing with a malign glance. "And you left this...this thing on my bed, Esmay."

I caught the dyed pink rabbit jacket before the 'thing' landed on the floor. Esmay handed me back my coat, and I helped her on with hers.

"I go," she winked, grabbing her bag off the gilded Empire sofa that forces one to sit like purse-lipped disapproving dowagers in the long undusted hall. "Much success to Madame."

"You're in a particularly happy mood, Calypso," I remarked to her disappearing back.

"Come up here and tell me what to wear."

Once this house was the only constant in Calypso's life. Once I resented this. Now, I am the constant. All of Calypso's husbands...and an occasional lover...had been coerced to live here. Other than for the installation of central air conditioning by husband number one, no trace of all those multi-personalities won out in this oompah symphony of brownstone.

Calypso stood dejected and irritable in silk, black, lacy, expensive lingerie, studying herself critically in the cheval glass. My cashmere robe from her puddled at her feet. Only God, she, and Esmay knew how long she had been trying on dresses. There was enough smoke in the air to fill a caucus room. Cast-offs lay everywhere. On the bed, empty boxes exploded mountains of tissue paper.

Once department store delivery vans collided in getting clothes to her that she might deign to buy. Now, when she's most insecure, she'll charge up to eighty or more dresses and return them all.

"I don't use fitting rooms" she told one department head.

"And it's not as if I wear them once as many do and try to return them. Some I know are a mistake before I take them from the box. So don't take that tone to me."

"Calypso, you shouldn't be so curt with Esmay. She's not competing for me with you."

"Esmay is a slut. She'd vamp a fireplug."

"That's not—"

"I know and she knows that my bark is worse than my bite. That's why she pays me no mind."

She twisted her head back to the mirror. Her face reflected sheer panic. She spoke to her reflection.

"I had Derek wax my entire body and then soaked in diluted peroxide. The age spots don't show in this light. All those years of savage sunning. Well, it was worth it at the time, I suppose. What say you?"

"That you've worked yourself into a tizzy for nothing. You were, are, and will always be, beautiful. Age does not lessen you, Calypso."

She smiled and came to me, kissing me, or rather almost kissing me, on the nose so as not to smudge the perfectly painted face. Her hair has been pulled back, loosely curling behind her ears and at the nape of her neck. I always wondered if she contrived her feline manners.

"Poor darling. I do run on. I'd kill my own Mother for a drink—"

"Calypso, stop."

"I would. I'd kill anybody but you for a drink."

I grunted and studied myself in her looking glass.

"The reception's being held in the Mt. Vernon room. I called the manager to ask him about the lighting. I'm best in soft pink, but he assured—"

"Did you tell him you know more about lighting than Marlene Dietrich did at eighty?"

"I suppose I do," she admitted, putting out the cigarette that had burned to the filter, "but what am I going to wear?"

"What about the dress on the floor?. I always liked you in that."

"I know, but there's a tiny grease mark on the bodice."

"Well, what about—"

"Let me show you this one."

"My God, Calypso, it will be you who'll catch your death."

"It would be worth it, don't you think?"

She lifted the dress above her head, letting it slide down over her, careful not to disarrange her hair or makeup. The piece of slinky bias-cut black satin hugged her body. I watched her. She lifted her skirt high to adjust her garter belt and smiled up at me as she bent to smooth her stockings before rising and squaring her shoulders..

"Too *jeune fille*?"

My groin growled at seeing her in this slip of a nothing being held up by rhinestone straps snaking across each shoulder.

"Do I look that silly? I must. I'll take it back—"

"No, Calypso, you don't look silly and don't return the dress. It's a killer. Tis a pity you were never a widow. What a magnificent one you would have made."

"Always a bride," she sighed, studying her double image. "And more's the pity that they're all surviving quite well without me. Even the ass who walked out when I told him only waiters wear wristwatches with black tie."

"You never told me that."

"I only just thought of him. He was so tiresome about it that I offered to buy him a pocketwatch."

"What a pair we are, Calypso."

"Yes *we* are," she agreed, putting down the tasseled atomizer, having scented her shoulders.

"Calypso."

"Yes."

"Don't wear any jewelry tonight."

"Nothing?"

"Only the diamond studs, then."

"Yes!!!!"

Her eyes gleamed. She went to the wall safe behind her

portrait which is never locked because she keeps losing the combination. Finding the earrings, her long fingers with the clear varnished half-moon nails nimbly inserted them into her pink lobes.

"I think I'll wear my blue fox."

"Yes," I nodded, coming to her.

"Darling, you'll muss my—"

"Fuck your lipstick."

"Welcome back, darling," she cooed with shining eyes.

That plundering kiss stabilized us. And Calypso ended up beaming her way through an evening of personal triumph amid soaring parrot-house praise that was exhausting but left her piercingly happy.

Everything considered, we weren't that late. Junior Leaguers were still wolfishly downing more than their fair portion of proffered food and drink. Calypso had swept past the Nutcracker-dressed doorman, strengthened and thankful for being ravaged by his admiring appraisal and ready to face a room where no one enters a large gathering anonymously without any degree of optimism, except when on friendly terms with everyone. Nor had the ex-honorable Mrs. Sully Ladson soured Calypso's night by accusing her of having slept with her still-honorable ex. Calypso's best party manners never served her better.

"I've met him, I'm sure, but—"

"You should be, considering he fucked you I don't know how many times."

"Was that during, before, or after he was married to you?" Calypso archly responded.

"Does that really matter?"

"*During* would have mattered to me, but I'm not you, am I? For I never slept around during any of my marriages."

Gently, I tried to slip from her stronghold. Nights of uninterrupted sleep without trips to the lavatory are a fading memory.

"Don't roll away just yet, darling," Calypso grumbled,

snuggling closer, her breath warm. "If I can forego a cigarette, so can you."

"Calypso," I whispered, kissing her tousled hair, "I need to urinate in the worst way."

My penis was beginning to feel as if it had been set on fire.

Her arm tightened, locking me, and I felt an unusual peace despite my discomfort.

"Not just yet, please. I have a confession to make."

"About what?"

"About Eddie."

"Eddie?"

"Um..."

"You mean Eddie Janchek?"

That sobered the moment. My breath whistled through my nose. My lips clamped in a thin line. I regarded her stonily.

"What have you been up to, Calypso?"

"Nothing," she assured and sighed from the effort.

Somewhere among all the clutter, Calypso's ormolu French clock clicked with sensual pleasure.

"When did you see him?"

"Recently."

"How recently?"

"Just recently."

"How did you find him?"

"I didn't. The detective I hired did."

I was breathing hard.

"You must have wanted to see him rather badly."

"I did at the time."

"And how much did finding him set you back?"

"Nothing. Absolutely nothing. The detective was...was a gentleman. He found Eddie in the telephone directory."

"The telephone directory," I repeated.

My sense of humor failed me. My hands twined in the eiderdown.

"To think I've spent all these years wondering where Eddie was, and all the time I could have dialed information for him. Eddie never moved away. He never left Anacostia."

I gritted my teeth and considered what she was saying.

"And Eddie never left Peoples."

Earlier, Calypso would have killed for a drink. I would have just as easily killed Eddie Janchek, though I realized the absurdity of this sudden resumption of jealousy on my part.

"Yes," she nodded. "He's a grandfather. Can you believe it? Three times. He has two children. A boy and a girl. He's kept his parent's house but sold the saloon. We talked a long time. His wife was at Mass. It was the anniversary of their other daughter's death. The one who died when she was only a week old."

I squirmed with pain.

"And?"

The pain burned and stung. I was beginning to cramp.

"And we agreed to meet."

"Where? At a hotel? Or did he come here? Is this a stale bed?"

It was she who rolled away to turn on the light. A white line appeared around her mouth. Her look was like a slap.

"Christ, don't be that way," she shouted, fully awake. "You don't have the right. Not with what you've been—talk about the double standard. When did I became Caesar's wife to you? He asked me to meet him for a drink. I told him I no longer drank. So we agreed on lunch. I met him at a place called Samantha's on—"

"On L Street. It's across from Brooks. There's a hotel next door. The Anthony, I believe."

"Goddammit, we didn't go to a hotel."

I couldn't stop myself.

"It would have been convenient."

"Stop it," she screamed, starting to cry.

"All right."

"We met there because the chain that bought Peoples, I forget..."

She lit a cigarette with shaky fingers.

"CVS."

"Yes," she exhaled. "The chain's opening a store on

Nineteenth Street and Eddie's doing the hiring. He's an area something."

I was sweating. A cold, clammy sweat.

"He's old," she sniffled.

"We all are, Calypso."

"No, I mean old. He's tired. Fleshy-faced. Worn-out looking. The fight's out of him. All that square-jawed cockiness is gone, but I would have slept with him. Slept with him out of pity. Only he wouldn't. He said it wouldn't be fair to his wife. She's always known about us. He cried. He's spent his whole life trying to get over me, and I got over him by seeing him again. Now I'll never have to dream again."

I reached out for her.

"I'm a prick, Calypso, I admit it."

"Yes, you are, but it does show you care. Do you? Or is it only wounded male ego?"

"I'll always care, Caly—."

I doubled over. My ribs felt broken, though I could breathe with no trouble. Calypso jumped out of bed, grabbing my robe.

"What's wrong? You...you aren't having a heart attack, are you?"

"No, I panted, but something—"

Wincing with effort, I stood up and had to sit down almost immediately. I tried again, standing limply. Amazingly Calypso was not going to pieces on me.

"Lean on me, darling. I'll get you to the bathroom."

I was having trouble keeping my balance. Had Calypso not been holding on to me, I would have tumbled forward. We made it and I shut the door, clutching for anything to hold onto. My insides throbbed, but nothing happened. The strain was telling in my legs. They trembled. I lowered the seat and sat down. I felt something. Something passing through but not urine. I raised myself to see. I saw blood. Clumps or clots of blood. Then even this stopped, and I thought my bladder was bursting. I splashed cold water on my face.

"Calypso," I called out. "I want you to call an ambulance.

Then call Hector to meet me at Sibley. Tell him my bladder's stopped working."

"I have," she was saying as I came out. She'd slipped on a teal silk dress and piled her hair into a Gibson-girl knot. "Hector's out-of-town. I left a message for the doctor on-call to meet us at Sibley."

"What about the—"

"I'm not leaving you."

She handed me my boxers. I was having trouble keeping my balance.

"One day," Calypso calmly remarked, putting on her raccoon coat, "you must tell me why you always button your shirts from bottom to top. I've often wondered."

I tried to smile.

It was dark outside, for the heavy trees cut off the light from the street lamp on the corner. We emerged from her door onto the steps that lead to the sidewalk. I estimated that Calypso's car was parked some twenty feet away by the alley. "Can you make it?" she asked. I shook my head and she left me to jerk the car into action.

The night was like a black sponge pressing against us. Only the moon watched over us. I finished tying my tie, snapped the collar pin shut and slumped back wearily. My collar was damp with sweat. Calypso lighted a cigarette and passed it to me, laughing.

"What's so funny?"

"We are, darling. We're so...so fundamentally proper that we could become curiosities. I'm not making fun of you."

"Blood tells, I guess."

"Yes, it does."

Calypso was hitting seventy. She ran her third red light, and I fumbled with putting on a seat belt, unprepared as I was to meet my Maker. More to keep talking than anything else, she asked again why I button from bottom to top.

"Did you ever read *Cheaper by the Dozen* about the Gilbrath brood?"

"You know the only books I read are yours, but I saw the

film. Mother took me to a matinee at the Apex. Afterwards, we walked over to Garfinckel's. She bought me new white kid gloves to replace the ones I'd ruined with red punch at your birthday—Christ, that was over forty years ago."

The car swerved. The walnut dashboard clock registered two-seventeen. She took a deliberate breath, "Mother's gone. The Apex is gone. Garfinckel's is gone. If you were—"

She bit her lip and pushed the thoughts away, but her hands clenched the leather-laced steering wheel. I reached over and put my hand over hers, making every effort to keep my own panic under control.

"I'm not gone yet, Calypso."

She cleared her throat with an attempt at carelessness.

"I'm all right."

"Sure?"

Her hands relaxed. She flexed her fingers.

"Now, what has that book got to do with anything?"

"The book was a biography written by Frank Gilbrath, Jr., on his father who was one of the first efficiency experts. It was he who determined that it's faster to button up than button down."

"That doesn't apply to marriage."

My eyes glazed over. I stared fixedly at the red taillight of the car far ahead.

"No, it doesn't, Calypso."

We said no more. I was certain my insides were rupturing by the time she swung past the box hedge and up the drive, braking abruptly at the tall glass doors of Sibley. Calypso ran ahead, ordering me to wait for a wheelchair. I thrust my head out of the open door, "Not on your life," and made my legs work to catch up with her in the lobby.

Calypso turned on the heels of her brown suede boots.

"Have it your way, but—Doctor!" She commandeered a furry man in blue scrubs whom I judged to be less than thirty. He showed more hair in the V of his top than I had on my entire body. "My...my *husband* may be dying. His bladder is bursting."

I was swaying in agony and stuttering when I was put on a

stubborn gurney that he somehow managed to maneuver into a curtained-off room in Emergency. Left behind was Calypso standing like a Valkyrie goddess.

"Don't let all this medical apparatus intimidate you," he said with a tired smile.

"I'm not, Doctor. Not even mildly. I was here last month for an operation."

"For what?"

Under the harsh light I saw that his eyes were red and his face lined.

"For an operation to remove a growth on my prostate. The growth proved to be benign."

"How was the growth detected?"

"Hector...Dr. Herrera found occult blood in my urine when I had a physical in November."

"Good man, Herrera."

"I think so...Doctor..."

"Ferguson. Call me Guy."

We shook hands as he pulled me up.

"All right, Guy."

"Here," he offered, "let me help you with your coat. Can you manage your shirt and tie?"

"Shouldn't I be unzipping?"

I was biting my lip.

"In due course. I want to give you an injection. Then you can undress. Great suspenders. Did you and your wife just leave a party?"

"Calypso's not—no, we just left her bed, and I told you that for a reason. Perhaps...perhaps it was too soon to resume, although I did wait a month short two days, and I wasn't supposed to drink, and I didn't until yesterday afternoon in Philadelphia. I forgot and had a straight double vodka."

"I'm surprised that she let you."

"I wasn't with her."

"I see."

Did he?

"Has this occurred before?"

"Never."

He rubbed my right arm with alcohol. The shot stung.

A redheaded nurse in a form-fitting uniform pushed back the curtain. She paid me no mind.

"Excuse me, Doctor—"

"Oh, nurse, would you get—"

"I'm one up on you," she twinkled. "I have his records here."

She placed my file on a bare metal table.

"Aren't you always?" he winked and she left liking that.

"Fine looking woman, Guy."

"Yes, she is," he winked again. "Can you finish undressing? Here, I'd better help you."

"May I keep on my socks?"

"If you like."

He took away my shoes and pants.

"Well, this is certainly a first."

"What is?"

"Tartan flannel boxers. Believe me, our usual patients don't arrive so well turned-out. They're even ironed and creased."

"Calypso and I are victims of having outlived our time, Guy."

My teeth chattered. It was cold being laid out in only a damp white cotton T-shirt and knee socks.

"That sounds like a line from one of your books."

"You've read my books?"

"A couple. Does that surprise you?"

"No, I'm flattered and encouraged. I was starting to believe I'd become *passe*. My newest book hasn't sold."

"It will, and when it does I would like to buy an autographed copy."

"Guy, I'll give you a copy or anything you want, if you get me out of this."

This time I couldn't keep the panic out of my voice. Just talking was torture, and he was beginning to frown.

"The injection isn't working. I'm going to have to catheterize you."

"You mean?"

"Yes, but you won't feel—"

"I don't care. Just do it."

He showed me the slender flexible tube that he was going to insert. I shut my eyes and waited. Nothing happened.

"Am I going to die?"

He cleared his throat and answered briskly, "No, but the clots are extremely large and there are so many. I'll have to recatheterize you."

"Then do, but hurry, Guy."

He did.

"Guy, nothing's happening."

"You're wrong. Turn your head and look down."

I did, but all I saw was blood coming through the tube and into the bag.

"You should be feeling a decrease in the pressure by now. Are you?"

All I could do was weakly nod. I lay there and watched the bag fill and be replaced with another.

"You have one helluva bladder. I'm stunned at the amount of fluid in your body. I'm going to have to put on a third one," he paused, "and I'm afraid you'll have to remain catheterized for several days due to the large number of clots."

That was a blow. I listened to his instructions and watched as he strapped a different type bag to my right leg. He helped me into an oversize pair of blue scrub pants and tied the drawstring. I felt like a sackful of old tennis balls walking back to admitting with his assistance, carrying my raiment in a plastic hospital bag.

Calypso was seated in a corner with Danny. They stood in tandem, their faces sharing an expression of inquiring anxiety.

"I knew Danny would appreciate being notified," Calypso explained.

"Dr. Ferguson, I'd like to introduce you to the two women in my life."

❦

# Chapter Twelve

*Wrung out, I lay thinking the day could only improve. Danny* rapped. I laughed tightly and stopped listening to the wind howl down the chimney and out to shake the dried hydrangeas in the zinc-lined bath, circa 1870, that Calypso had filled following the lamented demise of my last Jack Russell. The door opened easily on its laquered brass hinges. Danny put her head 'round, booming in high good nature, and entered in a quick tattoo of steps before coming to a full stop where one corner of the quilt sagged to the floor. I blanched at the sight of her bearing Aurora's inlaid mother-of-pearl *paper mâché* breakfast tray, long banished to the topmost shelf of the butler's pantry since Ursula's death.

"You're to eat this breakfast whether you want to or not. I went all the way to Georgetown to buy things you like."

Danny never fails to have a salutary effect on me. I grinned and eased myself up, taking care not to disconnect the tube from the bag, which chafed my right thigh like Gladstone's hair shirt. Straddling the tray across my lap, she unfolded a crisp napkin, arranging it bib-like on my chest. With a flourish she removed the lid from the covered bowl. My mouth gaped. Greedily, I scooped up a large spoonful of John McCann's Irish oatmeal that she'd topped with an over-generous portion of lemon curd, savoring its taste and texture. Such a simple, pleasant comfort, but such an expensive one, I realized. Frowning at yesterday's mail in the tray's pocket, I came to a sudden decision and waited for Danny to finish what she was saying.

"I opened the package from Hatchard's. One book wasn't

available, but you have a new Dick Francis and a new Colin Dexter. They're there in the right pocket in case you feel like reading, along with the paper."

"Uh, Danny, until the book sells I'd better develop a taste for Quaker Oats!"

Danny's eyes developed a puzzled squint.

"But you won't eat Quaker Oats."

"True, but I'd best start trying and also waiting for American editions of books to come out."

"You're worried, aren't you?"

"Hard to say," I ventured. "Shouldn't you be at Mrs...the shut-in, grateful though I am that you're here with me."

"I switched my hours with the new woman. Eat while it's hot. Calypso will be here tonight, whether you want her or not."

Folding her arms, Danny watched me like a benevolent despot. As I neared my fill, she spoke, "You're worried about money?"

I swallowed.

"Fewer people read nowadays, Danny. And those that do, are not reading me."

"We can make it."

I leaned my head back in the pillows, feeling like the lad in Stevenson's *The Land of the Counterpane.*

"You're a dear, cheery soul, Danny. I could not envision life without you."

She studied me, looking quite impenetrable before saying, "For sure, I can always see the bright side, unlike you and Calypso. She's rung twice by the way. I'll be forever in debt to her for calling me. Look, if worse comes to worse you could rent the carriage house. What with the garage, you could easily get twelve to fifteen hundred a month."

I slammed down my spoon.

"Don't even suggest such a thing," I exploded. "Not even obliquely. Where would you live, much less park?"

"In the attic and on the street, where else?"

"You'll stay where you are. We're together for the duration. Maybe I could get a teaching position. I like children."

"The children you like aren't found in a public school," she remarked in a voice of particular gentleness.

I suppressed a smile.

"Actually, I was thinking more along the lines of Friends or St. Albans, Danny."

"Oh, would they hire someone without a degree in Education?"

"I don't know, Danny. Colleges hire writers-in-residence. But I would prefer a more controlled environment."

"It won't come to that. Finish your breakfast."

Her false energy ebbed. When she pushed the bowl forward I noticed that her shoulders weren't as straight as when she had entered in her buff whipcords and heavy wool sweater.

"Danny."

"Yes."

"You're exhausted. I want you to go to bed."

"What if you should need me?"

"Danny, I'm not an invalid. Sleep in Ursula's room if you think I am. Leave these things. I'll take them down."

"If you say so," she agreed reluctantly. "What about that bag?" she grimaced. "Does it need emptying?"

"I can manage. I'm getting better at it. The first time, well, it was messy."

"I'll take care of it."

"No, you won't. Not that mess. I will. Now go. You're worn out."

"All right, but Trap wants to know what day you want him to put up the tree. The house is at its best at Christmas. It's the best time of the year for me."

I stared down at my empty bowl. She stood quietly waiting.

That I hadn't given 'the best time of the year' a thought for the first time in my life, I didn't want Danny to know. I stalled with, "Yes, it is, Danny. It's sweet old songs and bright new toys. Deep green trees and snow-swept skies. Icy mittens and child-wide eyes." Swept up by my own rhetoric, I told Danny to tell Trap that he could bring the tree the day after the tube was removed.

"Would you write that down for me?" she asked with a return of her natural vibrancy. "The part about snow-swept skies and icy mittens. Some of the best things you say you don't write down."

"If I can remember what I said, Danny."

"Well, write it down now so you won't forget."

She took away the tray and placed it on the William Morris chair. I couldn't fail but notice how pleasing the tray looked angled on the sprigged fabric.

"I will, but only if you'll get some rest."

"If you need me, I'll be in Ursula's room."

"I'll be fine. Now, shoo. You make me feel as if I couldn't sort socks."

"Have you ever?"

"That's beside the point, Danny."

"No, it isn't," she laughed, walking to the door in her faultless whipcords.

"Oh," she turned back, "there's rice pudding cooling on the kitchen table made from scratch with cooked rice, raisins and ground nutmeg. Don't know how you can eat the stuff. There's also a bowl of freshly made egg salad in the icebox."

"You make what's happened almost worth it. Bless you, dear Danny."

She gave me one of her neon smiles, "You're most welcome." What is truly handsome in Danny is her vigor.

When she closed the door, I reached for my robe and headed straight for the formidable burled armoire. Behind its fretted doors, lined with leaf-green silk, was my coat with a ticket stub stashed in the pocket. An address was written on the back. *Her* address. The address she gave me through the hurriedly rolled down taxi window before I watched her dwindle into the distance. The address was a Post Office Box.

A Post Office Box I questioned. What else was she hiding from her parents, besides the 'good' doctor?

My desk mocked and refuted my innate need for order. "What a God-forsaken mess," I said aloud. The haste of yesterday seemed an eternity ago. A coldness grew over me. I tightened the sash to my robe and raised the shawl collar. Wind, creeping through window frames, floated out the lace curtains. It was dejecting to see that the horizontal frieze between the architrave and cornice was puckering. I sat down, pushed aside Amanda's revised pages, and addressed and stamped an envelope before writing:

> Seeing you yesterday was my best Christmas present and for this I send you my thanks and appreciation. When shall you leave for your parents' place in Chester and when can I see you?
>
> I miss you,<br>Cheers

Finished, I sat back. My cigarettes were in the bedroom and Danny had not restocked the top desk drawer. I reread the missive, rubbed my eyebrows and noticed that the collection of foreign coins in the treenware pedestal bowl had been polished. A trickle of guilt reached my heart. I buried it, licked and closed the envelope, and went downstairs to greet the postman. He appeared quite taken aback at seeing me. "Danny's only resting," I responded, closing the door on him and the draft that whipped the blue scrubs around my ankles. I would write down the lines Danny wanted after emptying the bag.

I'm as weak as a cat I realized, climbing back into bed. I couldn't hold a book much less read one. I pulled the covers over me, secure in the womb-like warmth and darkness provided, and pushed my face into one of the pillows. Secure I was until I waked taut with fright. Pure panic, fright, isn't something that had visited my life often, but it was paying me a visit then. The second visit within twenty-four hours. My heart hit both sides like a pendulum at the dam-bursting pressure building inside me. I turned to lie prone. I turned again and met the sunlight brimming the room from the ceiling-high windows and I knew it was mid-afternoon, just as I knew I didn't need to check the bag to know that it was empty. Sweat was breaking out on my skin. I went to the bathroom and stood with a towel quiet against my face. Even upright nothing flowed. I took my face out of the towel and stayed at the window looking down on the garden. I tried to imagine it on a golden afternoon, and couldn't. Without leaves the trees were ragged, but how the walls had been softened by Danny's climbing vines and ferns that blurred the lines between perennial boarders and wall. Danny and I were about to go on an unexpected ride and this time I was dressed for the occasion.

"Are you his wife?" the admit staffer asked her.

"No, I'm his housekeeper, Mrs. Danvers."

"You pulling my leg?" the person scoffed.

"About what?" Danny stiffened.

"Housekeeper? Mrs. Danvers? It's made-up. Right?"

"Listen," Danny said coldly, shortly "I'm a housekeeper. His housekeeper. My name is Inga Danvers. My husband's name was—"

"Was Max," the woman pushed, playing with a pencil.

Danny does not suffer fools lightly. Flame swept into her face like straw catching fire.

"Max? His name was Warburg. Not that anyone ever called him that. Wally it was. You wanna see my I.D.?"

"That won't be necessary, I'm sure," was her pursed reply.

"I should hope not," Danny added, "He's the patient. He was here last night. I mean this morning."

"Yes, *we* know. The doctor is coming."

The doctor was a woman.

"Where's Dr. Ferguson?" I wanted to know.

"Sleeping. Can you make it without a wheelchair?"

"Yes, if we hurry."

"Good, come this—" she smiled sheepishly, "I forgot, you know the way, don't—"

"Poor darling," Calypso fog-horned, tearing through the

lobby like nothing on earth, cheeks wind-reddened, hair-flying. "I simply cannot believe this. Talk about *deja vu*." Faces made half turns. "God," she again fog-horned. What little life left in me was pressed out before she pulled off her gloves as if she were dismounting.

"Danny dear," she embraced almost affectionately. "I came as quickly as I — why he hasn't shaved. I had no idea his beard was white. Has this done it to him, Danny?"

Well, at least, I'll no longer need to creep from Calypso's bed to shave before breakfast.

"Danny!" the staffer almost choked. "I can't stand it."

Calypso regarded the woman seated behind the desk as one would a mosquito.

"Why yes, her name is Danny. Actually, it's Inga but we've always—"

"Then you must be the wife?" the woman painfully smiled.

Impatience struck at me at becoming a vagrant by association.

"Neither is my wife, madame, I'm not presently married. I'm a widower. I have been for quite a while."

"A widower!"

"Yes, goddamnit. Is that so unusual? This woman is—"

The person's focus of attention had quickly switched. Her jaw dropped. Her eyes had settled with the look of pointed inquiry I had come to expect when with Calypso.

"Weren't...weren't you Calypso Fox?" she blurted, ready to rush.

Calypso's nostrils quivered like a firehouse horse smelling smoke. Her voice becoming richly edged as she made the transition from trembling to bravado. "I was, and am. Disappointing isn't it after such a supreme beginning."

Faces full-turned this time. Danny's eyes rolled back. The woman seemed to shrink in her chair, almost to fade before our eyes. My heart squeezed against the background of Calypso's heavier anxieties. The young doctor whispered, "Who's Calypso Fox?"

Breathing more normally, Calypso swung about ready to send the woman standing next to me to the great drawing room in the sky.

"The question is, 'who the hell are you?'"

"The on-duty doctor and his doctor at the moment."

"Where's that tired, but sexy Dr. Ferguson?"

"Sleeping."

"With whom?"

"With no one, Miss Fox. We don't have time for that in ER."

"Well then, doctor, I suggest you see to your patient and stop asking questions that don't concern you."

As I struggled back toward equanimity, I tried not to think about not being recognized. Not that I cared, for I had little to say hampered as I was by what was about to be handled by yet another stranger.

I left Sibley Memorial Hospital in a kind of coma and remained so being wifed-to-death through three return visits. It seemed every doctor in ER had a pull on my parts in an attempt to flush out the blood clots. So grateful was I when the time came to leave behind the catheter in Hector's office, and for Calypso not pulling her magician's trick of turning into a bar for affirmation that I made known my plans for a Christmas party. Those invited would be from the Anglican Church School. No adults. No parents. With that decided, Trap, Danny, Calypso and I went at it full throttle. Danny's visions of sugar plums turned into fairy confections that Calypso equaled with favors for what would be an army, while Trap and I spent days and nights on ladders. It was a Christmas that twinned the rhetoric of the lines jotted down for Danny. The house, by its very spirit, had become animate in its effect on me and vitiated any need of *her*, as well as the pain and anger that had come from no reply to my note.

By Twelfth Night, I resolved I was better off without *her* anorexic soul. My life resumed. The days went by unfettered. I refused to think about what then. I was looking forward to my dinner with Amanda when I stopped tucking in my shirt to go answer the phone.

"He wants to meet you," *she* trumpeted without any preliminaries.

My mouth went dry.

"Who wants to meet me?"

"The doctor. My ex-boyfriend's father."

"Why the hell should he want to meet me? Do I need his seal of approval?" My voice faded away. "Bloody hell to the both of you."

"Are you quite finished?"

"For the moment."

"He wants to meet you because I've told him about you. He has no strings on me."

I barely stifled myself from saying, "Neither do I," but not from asking, "Isn't he jealous?"

"If he is, he's too big to show it."

When I made no comment, she placidly continued. "He's presenting a paper at Georgetown Medical School on the twenty-first. We're coming down on Sunday."

"Shall *you* be staying?"

"*He's* staying at the Grand Hyatt. *I'm* going back on the train. Well?"

"You didn't send me a Christmas card."

"I'm too young to send Christmas cards."

I suffocated my annoyance. Aversion rose thick in my throat. Her tongue clicked against the roof of her mouth in a show of impatience.

"Well?" she said.

"Well, what?" said I.

"Well, will you meet him?"

I felt as if I had lockjaw. After what was probably an hour to her, I decided why not.

"I'll meet him, but not here. The club has a rather decent buffet on Sunday evening. Tell him...I'll make reservations for *three* for six-thirty."

"Drinks would suffice."

"Not for me."

"Eros will be pleased."

"Eros?"

"Eros is his name."

"Eros as in Cupid?"

"Yes, I suppose it is." There was a little pause and, "Strange I never connected the two. His last name is Ruffin. Eros Ruffin."

Dry-throated, I refrained from making any sort of comment about my competitor's bow and quiver.

"How was your Christmas?" she inquired.

February is rather late to be asking, I ruminated, but replied with, "Sweet old songs and bright new toys. Deep green trees and snow-swept skies. Icy mittens and child-wide eyes. And yours?"

"Not like that. I couldn't wait to escape."

"Too bad."

"What news of your book?"

"It's at Random House. Have you finished what I gave you?"

"No, but I've made a dent."

"And?"

"And, so far I like it."

Instead of thanking her for the crumb, I said,

"I'll see you Sunday. I'm late for an appointment."

"So am I, goodbye."

As I slowly cradled the receiver, I recoiled at the lordliness of my largess with the kick of a shotgun on firing. Drinks would have indeed sufficed. About that, she was right. I was still mulling on this Sunday evening when I heard her voice sail up the stairwell and the temporary night man on the door tell them I was upstairs. Then there were two voices, each giving each other antiphonal replies. I crushed out my cigarette and listened to every firm footfall on the steps.

❦

# Chapter Thirteen

*Eros Ruffin wasn't tall. He wasn't short. He was a big heavy-*shouldered man with a simple heavy-full face and the clothes of a man down on his luck. He coughed frequently and touched his throat as if it hurt. He was fat, at least forty-plus pounds overweight with morose lines running from nose to mouth, but beneath bushy gray brows the opaque grey eyes were bright in a face so red and moist that it brought to mind a core cut from a watermelon. He jerked his head in salutation and sized me up lazily. What little hair he had reeked of Vitalis. Like a wave washing, like a tide rising, like any elemental surge, I thought, imagine kissing that, for the man was fast approaching seventy, if not already there. I had only a moment for shock for she was performing the introductions.

"Welcome to Washington," I said smoothly, shaking his hand and then pecking his young companion on her cheek. She was wearing the clothes she'd first charmed me in, and I the same blue suit, white shirt, and regimental silk tie. It was planned on my part. Was hers as well considered? The clocks ticked. His eyes wandered around the Federal reception rooms judging, probing the armchairs, sofas, and tables scattered in informal settings to create a rich ambiance of comfort and style. "Nice club you have here." John Adams' portrait, framed in hand-carved wood, looked down from above the fireplace where coals glowed red and piecrust mahogany tables gleamed in lamplight. They both seemed too inhibited to speak. He gave a dry laugh. "Thanks for having us."

"Yes," she reinforced.

"My pleasure," I smiled at good manners all around and motioned for Mary before we sat down.

His wide shoulders lifted, "Who's the bloke?"

I sat in my chair at the apex of alertness, laughing at myself for monumental in my mind I had made him and our meeting. "President Adams. John Adams. He spent the night before his inauguration here."

"Impressive history," he coughed and I saw how her face registered concern. Would she have been as concerned about me if she'd known?

Eagerly I forced the words, "I suppose, but what's your pleasure?"

"Scotch and ice, thanks. My throat feels a little dusty."

Mary's, "Punch, Glenfiddich or Balfour, sir?" was followed by abrupt flat silence. Eros Ruffin's mouth took on a three-cornered grin.

"That's an impressive selection, ma'am." He rubbed his blue-shaven chin. "Balfour, and make it a double while you're at it."

Mary dimpled, finished taking our orders and left. My guest of honor cocked his head 'round and commented on the deathly emptiness surrounding us by way of, "Sunday must be a slow night."

"It's early yet, but attrition and arthritis is taking its toll, not only here, but in all clubs. Still, it's an escape from the noise and unpleasantness of M Street and what has happened to Georgetown."

"I wouldn't know, not belonging to a club." He studied the party of six coming in before pulling out a pack of Winstons, and settling back. "Is it okay?"

"Absolutely! I'd resign if I couldn't smoke."

I moved one of the small pewter ashtrays toward him and looked blankly at my other guest.

"My son, however, has recently joined the Metropolitan Club. Did you know he lives here?"

"No," I lied.

"Going on two years. George is with Hamilton and Hamilton. You know it?"

"Who doesn't. The law firm founded by Alexander Hamilton." I stole a glance. Her face was unreadable. "If I'd known, I'd have included him."

"George wouldn't have come. We don't...well, let's say all that fancy education I gave him changed him. And then there was the matter of— a fancy education didn't affect my daughter...or help her...for that matter. She's twice divorced and works for me as my receptionist."

"But your son...he'll be at Georgetown to hear you, certainly?"

Harsh words grated from his throat.

"George doesn't even know I'm in town. We...we don't communicate, but that's all right. I did the best I could by him. I sent him the money to join that club. Ten thousand dollars and paid the dues for a year. My old man never saw that much money at one time in his whole life. Let George enjoy life, I say. This is it. Life's not a rehearsal, and you don't get a second chance."

His chortle was not a joyful chuckle. And, to what he'd made me privy, embarrassing. I heaved a silent sigh at seeing Mary fast approaching.

"Cheers," he toasted, sipping his whiskey.

I saluted and swallowed. Little by little the strings that govern me began to pull me together. I studied my other guest's face and felt overwhelmed. There were so many things I wanted to say to her. Christ, but I go to pieces around her. What else besides that look of concentration was on her face? Was it pride? Pride in him? Pride in the balding man wearing unpolished brown shoes with cotton laces who fucks his son's girl while his acrylic socks sag around his ankles? In her eyes, he wears a full-length halo. Her aureoled knight punched out at me with one of his fingers saying, "I don't know how much you already know about—"

"Nothing," I interrupted, finding a semblance of voice at the import of those words.

Instead of continuing, he sat as if he had been pulled aside to some extraneous thought. "Well, I'll tell you," he said after awhile with a sly half-smile on the underslung lip. "I came from Falcon. Falcon, North Carolina. Ever heard of the place?"

"No," I nodded.

"No one has. It's a dirt-poor place about fifty miles from Raleigh. I grew up there. My old man was a sharecropper. Ever heard of one of them?"

This time I nodded, "yes." I felt like a ventriloquist's dummy.

"I'd never been more than five miles from the farm until the day I finished high school and I boarded the bus for Raleigh. I've never been back. I enlisted in the Army. They sent me to Fort Lewis in Seattle, Washington, and after boot camp, I was shipped to France, then we pushed on to Germany. When the war ended, I enrolled at Columbia on the G.I. bill. Finished sixth in my class and was accepted by the med school. From the day I was born I was determined to become a doctor and goddamnit I am. I did my residency at Thomas Jefferson in Philadelphia and decided to stay on. I've done all right. Got a house in Chestnut Hill and a little place in center city that I keep for sentimental reasons. My wife and I bought it with our first real money. She was my nurse, the head neurosurgery nurse that is, and then my wife."

His lids dropped over the aluminum eyes. The handful of crunchies that he took were chomped with gusto before he cozily continued.

"You're the only author I've ever met. Wish I could say that I've read your books. My wife has, or says she has. She's a member of a book club. The only books I read are medical ones. George has read you though, as I recall. Have you done anything recently?"

"Actually, I'm expecting a favorable decision from Random House anytime."

"Writing is hard for me. I don't envy your line of work. My daughter helped a lot on the paper I'm presenting. Those little statues on the mantel are 'MISSEN,' aren't they?"

"Sorry, what?"

"'MISSEN,' those statues over there are 'MISSEN,' if I'm not mistaken."

"Ah, I don't know much about china."

"My wife and I collect things. We recently bought an Audubon at auction." The stress on the pronouns suggested overwhelming pride, and his face showed the same possessive gratification. "It belonged to a Wanamaker. Kinda hate to have something like that cut down just to fit the—"

"You bought a what?"

"An 'Audubon' rug."

"Oh, yes. Ah, why not fold the borders under? After all, who would notice once the furniture is placed?"

"That's a swell idea. I'm going to find out from that decorator fella hired by my wife why he didn't think of that. Thanks. Thanks a lot. Say, would you mind my asking where you buy those oxford cloth shirts with rounded collars?"

"I had them made at Brooks ten or more years ago."

"They're classy. Real class. Is that a real gold safety pin?"

"Brass, Dr. Ruffin," was my disclaimer. "Brass. And brass-plated at that."

I was saved from what would have been a dreary discourse on shirts by Dee leaning over to say the table was ready.

"Shall we?" I said with a rush.

Dr. Ruffin sucked his glass dry before saying, "Sure."

"We can go through here and down. Watch your step at the landing."

"This is what I call handsome," he paused, stopping to admire the view of the dining room from where we stood while I steeled myself to his whistling britches. Dr. Ruffin was either very happy or very nervous, but I chose to believe he was happy, for other than for she of decent people, I had nothing against him.

"In colonial times this was known as the great hall and was where assemblies were held."

He listened intently.

"This stuff interests me. Go on. What about the wallpaper?

I know the chandeliers are 'Waterfield.' I have two hanging in Chestnut Hill."

"All I know is the paper was handpainted in China especially for the room. It was restored last year. The carpet, which is new, was installed just before Thanksgiving. It was designed by Stark Weavers. I know that only because Dee told me."

"Dee?"

"The evening manager. The woman who told me our table was ready."

At table, my largess continued. I ordered wine, something I never do. I ordered right after he told me they drove by my house on their way to the hotel and also Tune-Inn. My placing him between us gave him an unimpeded view of the room. His eyes took in a table properly linened, while the thick, creamy bisque with sherry *a la* Rosa Lewis, was deftly served. Boldly he turned over the soup spoon. Dinner was going to proceed with the speed of old jazz records. When we returned from the buffet he chummily wanted to know my plans for Monday.

"The usual. Writing. That is how I make my living," I reminded him.

"I guess I couldn't persuade you to meet me at Tune-Inn for lunch tomorrow?"

Listening to the pianist doing justice to *Honey Bun*, I considered how deeply I wished to be a part of this unholy trinity. "She's my girl / I'm her guy / She's my little sweetie pie / Get a load of honey bun tonight." The words applied to them, not to me.

"Thanks, but I rarely lunch out. It breaks the flow, especially if I'm on a roll."

"I'll call you after the lecture in case you change your mind." He paused, waiting for me to make some suitable response. "I have your number."

"You do? Oh, yes, I guess you do," I said looking at her. I decided all I had to do was let him go on talking. "By the way, what is the subject of your paper?"

"Cardiac thrombosis. Strokes. Wouldn't mean much to you."

"Only if I had one," I replied, tasting the wine and approving, which was a joke, considering my being a tawny port or ruby claret man.

"True," he laughed.

Toward the end of dinner, Dee, all bustle and business, came by and I took the time to inquire about Rodney with a quiet aside.

"Improving daily I'm happy to report. He appreciated your card. I'll be sure to tell him you asked. Enjoy the rest of your evening."

"Is Rodney her husband? " the girl I shared inquired. Her question caused rising brows and headshakes from the nearby tables.

My smile was *pro forma*.

"Rodney's the doorman."

"Oh," she said, the one syllable a gargle in her throat.

I was thinking if I were going to be able to grab a moment alone with her when, with a sharp glance back over his shoulder, my guest of honor whispered, "Is this a restricted club?"

My embarrassment deepened.

"I wouldn't know, Dr. Ruffin, not being on the board."

His heavy face assumed conscious lines of doubt and bemusement. "Say," his elbow nudged, "that man over there, isn't he Senator—?"

"Beats me, Eros. All politicians look alike. Like newscasters and babies. Only I like and trust babies. More coffee? Brandy, perhaps? No?"

With a headshake he glanced at his wrist watch, bringing time into being, "Better not. Either might keep me up and I'm keyed up enough over tomorrow. I'll leave you two to talk and head back to the hotel. About lunch, I'll call you and if you can't, let me know when you'll next be in Philadelphia. It's taken me seventy years to get to this beautiful city and I thank you for putting up with me. My son will be real impressed when his mother writes him."

In the emptiness succeeding their leaving, I felt spent. I rolled a piece of hard candy in my mouth and paced the reception hall not seeing anything until he reappeared, wearing an ill-fitting dark navy raincoat.

"I want to—" he shyly began.

"Ready, Eros?" she broke in, coming from the side hall. She looks at him the way she never looks at me. Familiarly, she linked her arm with his.

"Just about, I was say—"

She fussed like Danny about his hat.

"Put on your cap, you know how easily you catch colds."

"It's in my pocket. I'll put it on outside." He moved his hand over his head as if he still had hair.

"She's about the only one who worries about this shining plate, but thanks again for having us and also for making a dream come true."

"Which was?" I asked, entertained.

"You see, when I was a boy picking tobacco I dreamed about one day making my own ice cream sundae and putting on all I wanted of everything with no one to stop me. Well, tonight I did."

"I had the same dream, Eros."

"You must have, for you made yourself two, but you never picked tobacco. You appreciate things more in life after that."

"I suppose so, Eros. Call me tomorrow. I'll try to make lunch."

"I'm not being cheap mind you. I'll do right by you the next time you're in Philadelphia, but this one," he winked, "has gone on so about the place that I—"

"I understand. Believe me. I could eat at Tune-Inn everyday if I didn't have to worry about my thickening waistline."

"When you reach my age you won't have to worry. Good night. Hope to see you tomorrow."

"Good night to you, Eros, and good luck—though I'm sure you won't need it."

"Thanks."

We firmly shook hands and she went out to the street with him saying, "I'll be right back."

It hit me that they were the perfect complement. For he

was the performer and she the audience, and in my life I have been the audience and all the others the performers. Now I have become the performer and she hasn't decided whether she wishes to be my audience.

When she returned to where we'd begun the evening, I was seated in a secluded corner by the fire. Breathless, she hurried toward me pushing back her hair. "Everything was perfect. You, the dinner..." She laughed shakily. I watched her face as she leaned down to kiss me. Her eyes half closed, her lips parted, her tongue-tip peeking out. Her lips were soft, gentle, but grew in hardening pressure and my breathing came heavy, fast as her fingers grazed the nape of my neck. I loved her mouth. I savored her tongue before it slid in my mouth like it belonged there. And her response was to pull away.

"Eros's never really been with anyone like you. What's this?"

"Club soda for you. Port for me. Or would you rather I'd ordered a brandy?"

"You have an amazing memory."

"I'm a writer, remember?"

"I haven't forgotten."

She curled those sweet young legs in the chair like a long child. Above her head, the portrait vouchsafed for her. Silently I linked fingers with hers, wondering where to begin for there was not much thought behind what I had to say, except desire.

"He has a name now," I began.

"Yes, his name is Eros. And I know he talks too much and his malapropisms are laughable, but he's the *real thing*."

"So am I."

"If you *weren't*, I wouldn't be fooling with you, but you were never grandfather disadvantaged, were you?"

"Is this a strike against me? A black mark in your book?"

"Of course not. Nor in his. Eros likes the real thing. What most impressed him was your courtesy. Not just your manners or politeness, but plain courtesy."

"Would you like to define that?"

"Well, Eros is right of course, you have beautiful manners,

but so do a lot of men. One can be taught manners or pick them up along the way, but one can't be taught courtesy. Courtesy comes from inside a person. You have the ability to make the other person feel that no matter who they are you're terribly interested in them. Eros thinks you're pre-Depression. Like the owner of the big white house on the hill back in Falcon who always took time with him and paid for his visits to the dentist."

"Your friend understands me far better than you. I choose to be what I am. I don't lead. I don't follow. So where do we go from here now that I've passed all the tests with flying colors?"

"What do you mean?"

She took her hand back and mine felt empty.

"I believe the question is fairly obvious. We're going nowhere slowly."

"Everything is perfectly normal," she diagnosed with an impersonal, cut-off coolness, putting down her glass.

Cautiously, I said, "I don't think so."

Around her mouth and eyes defensive muscles hardened. Slowly the face changed, becoming icy, indifferent.

"Don't try to glamorize something hackneyed."

I stopped to recover from this new dispiriting blow.

"All you really want to know is when you're going to get some sugar from my bowl."

In my mute misery I thought her breath smelled like dead fish.

Having made her point, she hastily attempted a poured-on apology.

"I shouldn't have said that," she admitted.

"No, you shouldn't have," I said with a rush, "because it shows how utterly indifferent you are to my feelings."

Her face stayed closed.

"I disagree. I can't be rushed. Eros *needs* me. He's not well. We think—"

"We?"

"His daughter and I believe Eros—"

"You and his daughter are friends?"

"Yes, close friends. Does that surprise you?"

I shot Dee a 'do not disturb us' look, and she backed away.

"Does his daughter know?"

"Of course."

"Jesus."

"It's complicated, like you said about, Calypso," she answered coldly. "I don't have time to explain. I'll miss my train."

"So," I countered barely stirred.

"So? So what?"

"So it's not as if you don't have a place to sleep. Three in fact, if George were included. How long am I to remain Robin Goodfellow?"

"Who?"

"Puck."

Red lanterns flared in her eyes.

"Why don't you go fuck yourself?"

What a neat, little, lethal number she was. If she had shouted those words, it could have been simply an outburst. But they were said stubbornly, with intentness, while I sat stock-still. My entire interior seemed to empty, as those sweet young legs walked out, and along the base of my skull I had a tingling as if small hairs were curling into corkscrews. I guess that washed me out.

༄

# Chapter Fourteen

*I looked at my watch when the call came. It was eight minutes* past one. He was coughing. Coughing and apologizing.

"Sorry about that," he opened. "Sorry also about having to back out of our going to Tune-Inn. Something came up. I'm flying back. I've already checked out, but...ah...I want to ask you something."

"Ask away, Eros."

That I was disappointed, I didn't want him to know.

"Eros?"

He was coughing again.

"The thing is this. Have you learned anything about this preternatural interest of hers in old men?"

That made me laugh.

"I was hoping you could tell me, Eros. You of all people should know. Perhaps she suffers from gerontophilia."

"What's that?"

"A person who is sexually attracted only to older people."

"That's a disease?"

"Not in your case. Better that than gerontophobia."

"What's that?"

"A person who's afraid of older people."

"Well, if that's the case, you're too young for her. And she's the one who came on to me. I didn't take her away from George."

"You didn't?"

"Hell no, I didn't. Is that what she told you?"

"No, I just assumed."

"Well, you assumed wrong. I take anything that's offered,

but not my son's girlfriend. It was all her idea. Listen, I slept with her for two days before I touched her. We were at her parents' farm in Chester. She planned everything. I thought she was a virgin."

Did I believe what he was saying? I stared awhile at the carpet.

"Are you still there?"

I answered without looking up, "Ah, yes, Eros."

"Girls like her weren't meant for men like you. You listen to me."

"I'm listening. Why?"

I reached for a cigarette. Eros was being heavy on the avuncular.

"Because she's a hurricane not having any place to go. That business of hers is going nowhere, too, what with that sister-in-law cheating the hell out of her. But the main thing with her is that, while she may look the part, she's just plain not comfortable in the world you were born to. Neither is my daughter for that matter. But George, by God, he takes to it like a duck to water. Not that he's like you. You never think about it. I knew that right off. That's why I like you. George, well, he thinks about it all the time. Me? I don't give a rat's ass. I got what I want. Don't get me wrong. She likes you well enough, though she fights it, and I'm not jealous. It's not like I'm screwing her. I gave that up when my wife found out. Found out and left me. After six months she decided we were too old to start over. She forgave me, but she sure as hell ain't forgetting. And no way was I planning on taking me a new wife. Now that shifty attorney, Riley, she's fucking, who's the same age as her father..."

"Eros," I broke in, "I wouldn't want you to miss your plane."

"You pissed at me?"

"No, Eros, it's only that I don't want to hear anymore just now."

"I'm telling you this because I—"

"I know, Eros."

My voice trailed off, and his took over.

"You will call me when you're next in—"

"Of course, goodbye."

Unmanned with anguish, I heard the hunger in the wind's sightless progression. In this melancholy mien, I could easily die of wasted love. I crushed out what was left of my cigarette and started another before dialing Calypso.

"Surprise!"

"Surprise is right, darling. Oh, my god, you...you haven't clogged again, have you?"

"No, but I've...I've plummeted to my professional nadir, Calypso."

"My last doctor, the one in Stockbridge, told me that the good thing about a nadir is that any subsequent motion is inevitably upward."

"Unless the pendulum has stopped."

"Darling, it's only paused to gather momentum."

"You can be strangely comforting at times, Calypso, but I've written my last book. I'm written out."

"I don't believe you for one minute. However, if you are, why not ghostwrite my autobiography. It would give you a well-earned break."

"Ghostwriters don't write, Calypso. They...they, well, rearrange selected memories. Are you serious about an autobiography?"

"Of course. It would be my way of becoming immortal."

"Have you thought of a title?"

"I have."

"Let me guess. *Id and I*."

"Hardly."

"Well, then, what about *Very Fond of Men*."

"It's true, I'm not ashamed. I *am* very fond of men. Once I had them lined up like bon bons in a confectioner's box. All women aren't fond of men, even those who indulge in that unnatural state of matrimony. No, my title would be simply *Calypso*, done in that florid script lettering that was used for *Gilda*."

"*Gilda?*"

"Rita Hayworth's legacy to the world. The film where she sang *Put the Blame on Mame, Boys*, and stripped by peeling off her elbow-length black satin gloves before eloping with Aly Khan. I would be the L in *Calypso*. The same as Rita was in *Gilda*."

"You became jaded at an early age, Calypso. No one would have thought it to look at you then. You appeared to be an angel."

"You always had a sympathetic imagination."

"I did?"

"And do. What about my book?"

"Buy a dictaphone, have what you record transcribed, and I'll do the edit."

"Promise?"

"Promise. Oh, Calypso—"

"Yes?"

"Seriously, what about *Survivor* as a title?"

"YES," she affirmed, "With a subtitle reading *The Memoirs of the Last Great Debutante and How She Found God With a Glue Gun*."

"You may have a winner at that, Calypso."

"Truly?"

"Truly."

"I'll buy one of those machines Saturday. It will be so easy to talk as I work. Also, it may improve Esmay's English, and I'll be the V's in survivor."

"Wait until next week."

"Why?"

"Let's go to Jimmy's party. We can catch an early train and Bud can drive us out."

"But you said you had no interest in going to Jimmy's murder mystery weekend at *Andalusia* when the invitations arrived."

"Can't I change my mind?"

"What's really eating you?"

"Nothing. Don't you want to go?"

"Of course, I do."

"Well, then, I'll arrange things and call you back."

Had what Eros told me changed anything? Absolutely not. On returning Monday afternoon, I decided to start again and did by calling her office. She answered.

"Hello."

"Hello, yourself. Hold on while I switch you to my office." I waited.

"Bad time?" I asked when she picked up.

"As good a time as any, I suppose. Good, too, that you ran off our receptionist. We would have had to let her go this week anyway."

"Things that bad?"

"Yes, they are."

"I'm sorry."

There was a pause.

"Are you?"

"Of course I am. Why wouldn't I be? And why would you think, much less say such a thing?"

"I don't know. Because I felt like it, maybe. Excluding Danny, exactly how many women have you known who've worked or had careers? Certainly not those purposeless debutantes you've spent your life playing with."

"You're not purposeless."

"I wasn't a debutante," she answered with a change of tone.

"Is that what's bothering you or the fact that your business has gone sour?"

"Who told you that?"

"You did."

She laughed.

"I guess I did. I'm in a bitchy mood."

"You don't say."

"I do say. I don't know why you pursue me. Why you would want me."

"Yes, you do. I—"

"Don't...not now. Wait until I can sort things out."

"And when shall—"

"I'm going to be in Baltimore on Wednesday. We could meet."

"What time?"

"Fivish, I should think."

"What hotel?"

"Hotel?"

"Where are you staying?"

"I'm not staying in a hotel. I'm coming...and going back on a train."

"In that case why not meet me at the—"

"Why don't you meet me this time?"

"Fine. Where?"

"The Brass Elephant. It's on—"

"Charles Street."

"You know the place?"

"Yes, the restaurant's across the street from the Maryland Club and an easy walk from the station. I'll come up on MARC and back on Amtrak. We'll have more time that way."

Our conversation left me soberly content and as gratefully optimistic as a faithful swain until, with a bolt, I recalled the invitation Calypso and I had for Wednesday afternoon. Moving quickly, I rifled the footed silver toast rack used for mail. Sure enough there it was:

> *The Commandant, Naval District Washington*
> *requests the pleasure of your company*
> *at an acceptance ceremony*
> *of Polar Exploration Memorabilia*
> *from the family of Rear Admiral Richard Blackburn Black*
> *Navy Museum*

The time was one o'clock. Damn. And Aviza, my favorite godchild, is his granddaughter. Perhaps...Esmay answered after an eternity.

"I giving Madame her hot oiled massage. Esmay no time to talk."

"I wasn't calling you, Esmay." My teeth ground with

impatience. "Much as I do enjoy our infrequent conversations, it is Madame with whom I wish to speak."

"You make beeg joke with Esmay, right?"

"Just hand Madame the phone, Esmay. This is important."

"Si."

"Sa."

"Missing me, are you?" Calypso yawned seductively. "Why not sleep over now that everything is performing so well? I'm not in the mood to create and I'm too old to propagate. I can do it for fun, thank God."

"I'll drop by after dinner. Want any leftovers?"

"Darling, after our weekend at Jimmy's, I may never eat— ouch Esmay, that hurt. How many times must you be told that I bruise easily?"

"Calypso, about Wednesday."

"Yes."

"'The Pink' is going to be in Baltimore—"

"As much as I'd love to see Pinky, I simply can't, darling. A charming man with a Jewish name from Bergdorf's is flying in to discuss featuring my things on its seventh floor over dinner at the Four Seasons. I thought I told you."

"You didn't. 'The Pink' will be disappointed. I'm meeting him at five."

"That's pushing it what with the ceremony for Dick."

"Not if you don't start believing you're back at an Annapolis tea dance with all those midshipmen that are sure to be swarming all over the place."

"*Moi?*"

"*Moi.*"

"Nasty thing. I'll make you pay for that tonight."

I played along.

"Promise?"

"In spades, darling, but I'll control myself tomorrow and we'll tear away as soon as politely possible. I'll even drive you to Union Station."

I don't know whether I could handle this much guilt.

"You needn't go that far, Calypso. I know you go to pieces in heavy traffic."

"Ungrateful beast. Don't refuse my self-sacrificing offer. Try finding a taxi at the Navy Yard."

"That's true."

"Esmay, that's divine. I could simply float away."

I could see Calypso stretched languidly on her padded massage table.

"Oh," she seemed barely able to get the words out. "Maybe you should bring something."

"For instance?"

She added dreamily, "Something for us to eat under the sheets. Perhaps a large tin of Poppycock."

Unlike Calypso, Danny let me know with a clouded face, before she slammed down and spattered the dessert bowl of floating island, that 'The Pink's' two-day visits come around the middle of August.

"And lucky for you," she continued, with what I thought was a momentary flicker of her eyelids, "that my memory's better than Calypso's except for when it comes to herself. You may tell that choo-choo toy of yours that I haven't forgotten about the napkin."

Through no fault of Calypso's, I arrived in Baltimore thirty-five minutes late. The sky was turning purple and it was starting to snow. Panting from the three-steps-at-a-time climb from the platform, I blatantly ignored a stalled queue by jumping into a taxi and slamming the door on the justly warranted, but pointedly rude remarks being hurled at me. Any one of them would have done the same, I justified. I was in love.

"The Brass Elephant," I wheezed to the driver. "Know the place?"

"Yeah."

"Good."

"She must be some filly, judging by the way you're sweating," he surmised rightly, looking at me in the rear view mirror.

I *was* sweating. Beneath a camel's hair coat, I was wearing a Scottish wool houndtooth jacket of autumn colors, and the

tailored World War II gaberdine pants that had belonged to
Fitz Fox, Calypso's father, Fitzgerald, who before marrying,
drove his twelve-cylinder yellow Packard convertible across the
country from Harvard to the Biltmore in Santa Barbara getting
laid at every country club or roadhouse along the way.

"She is that, driver, and more."

"Then she'll wait. Relax. Lower the window. Have a smoke,
if you like."

"I like."

"Don't mention it. Our so-called government's turning
this great country of ours into a Gestapo nation."

"You're a real tonic," I told him.

"So I've been told," he laughed.

And so he was. So much so that I was able to gaze
appreciatively at the stately portal of Charles Morton Stuart's
nineteenth century townhouse as the taxi came up on this lone
survivor that houses the Brass Elephant. Carved stonework
scrolled up to an escutcheon above a great oak door that was
being pulled ajar as I tipped the driver. She stood confidently
upon squares and squares of black and white marble before
stepping back to give entry to a man, bypassing a beautifully
polished bell-pull, a 'buzz off, buster' expression. My heart
pounded. My pulse raced. My hands felt clammy. If this weren't
love I'd better see a doctor.

She straightened my bow tie approvingly and slipped her
hand through my arm, asking, "How are you?"

And I said, "Not too shabby," kissing her lightly and
determined to keep things light. The trick was to try to ignore
her little girl voice.

"Sorry about being late."

She looked impossibly wonderful and all-American. And
she knew it.

"There was a power failure at Union Station."

The scent of her quivered my nostrils.

"The train doors locked."

She was savvy enough to understand her appeal and what
she was doing to me.

"I couldn't call or get off to smoke."

How much longer was she going to keep me guessing?

"Then I stupidly forgot Charles Street was one way the wrong way."

Her, "I thought I'd been stood up," was said with a society smile.

"Not likely," I assured over the brassy laughter coming from the bar.

"I asked if you'd called and was told you had but only to make a reservation."

"Did they tell you I made two?"

"Two?" she frowned.

"One is in your name, in case you didn't. Both are in the Teak Room."

"I didn't," she admitted. "We'll cancel mine. You're so unconsciously organized that what you do is nothing more than a reflex."

I liked the 'we.'

"Was the trip down...ah, fruitful?" I managed, watching her keenly.

She sank into her chair, abandoning her drink. Her small fingers curling and uncurling themselves nervously. When she responded she spoke sincerely and earnestly. All that brave defiance was gone.

"No, and the business is going downhill."

"But you aren't," I put in warmly. "This courage of yours will never desert you."

She touched my lips with her fingers.

"It's the waiting. The wondering and expecting it to happen. On top of everything else, I got myself into this ridiculous situation by trying to please my family. My brother actually and father invested too much—oh, it's all so complicated and my sister-in-law is money-grubbing and besides cheating me, she's cheating on my brother. This new partner she's bringing in is her lover and all everyone in the family wants is peace."

"What do you want?"

"OUT!" she answered quickly.

"Out to do what?"

She looked up, her face serious.

"To be free. To be free of all of them."

No one is free, I added mentally.

"Free to do what?"

"Free to move out. Free to go to business school. Stocks interest me. Mother thinks it queer. She wants for me what you want for me." Her face flushed. Her unhappy eyes met mine. "Just give myself up to the sweeter things, but that doesn't add any meaning to existence. To mine at least." She gave me a crooked, vacant smile. "You think there is something not quite normal about me, don't you?"

My eyebrows raised. I regarded her curiously. "Not quite normal?" Not about what she wanted, certainly. The New Woman is bombarded with this. About Eros and the others, I wasn't sure. However, that wasn't the question.

"Are any of us quite normal?" I answered dryly. "And I don't see that it would take an amendment to fulfill your rosy hopes."

"You mean like an amendment to the Constitution? Like a law to amend the blues?"

"Yes, in a way."

"No, it wouldn't take an amendment. Only money."

"Is that a problem?"

"You can afford to be relaxed," she threw out as a counterargument, "I can't."

My jaw clenched. I looked into her unblinking eyes, but said nothing as she continued.

"I hate having to hurt father and then take his money. So I'm letting my sister-in-law and her...her partner buy me out, but will not take a lump sum. I plan on drawing a weekly salary while I decide what I am going to do with my life. I'll also be moving out of Chestnut Hill."

"To where?"

"To center city."

"But, where in the city?"

Some sense of being under scrutiny seemed to be all that

reached her. She read my meaning. Her smile assumed the pity of the sophisticate for a country cousin.

"You've been talking to Eros."

Again she wore her armor.

"How is Eros?" I finessed. "What was his emergency?"

"His wife tripped over that damned rug and broke her arm, but seeing as you're so concerned over my living arrangements, I'll tell you. I'll be renting a bedroom in an apartment. The apartment belongs to a woman who happens to be a professional student. She has I don't know how many degrees, but at the age of thirty-three she's applied and been accepted to med school. Her name is Andrea. I'll give you the address and number when it's official. You'll be pleased. I'll be living near the Racquet Club."

Knowing when I've been put in my place, I said, "Shall we order?"

"Yes, will you motion for the waiter. I always have trouble with that and you do it so well. I must learn how to perfect what you do so effortlessly and on the first try. You really are the perfect specimen for this white elephant. Like the brass bell-pull, you fit, which is why we're here."

Somehow what she said managed to convey patronization. I eyed the detailed designs created by Moroccan artisans for the Teak Room and the pair of marble mantelpieces sculpted by Henry Rinehart. Less sympathetic souls prefer extensive gutting and sheetrock.

"When you're older or once you're in a furnished room you'll understand that beauty is not a mere accessory to life, it is an absolute necessity."

She shrugged impatient shoulders and we ordered. Following this, I became the recipient of an uneasy smile.

"I never dreamed you would have known of the Brass Elephant."

"I don't know why?" I said lighting her cigarette.

"The Maryland Club is more your speed, I guess. I was invited there once."

"You should have gone."

"Why?"

"If for nothing more than the frosted crab."

"Which is?"

"A chilled soup."

"If he asks me again, I will."

I felt my face go blotchy over my tan.

"Oh, God, I'm sorry. You're so...so...He's just a boy. You would like him, he has an inherited face. It's his father who's the member." Her breath caught in a brief hiccup. "Christ—look I've never met his father. Nor am I planning to— How's your drink?" she asked hastily taking hers.

"Smooth. Smooth as silk. The place has a damn fine bartender."

"I think so."

Fishing for one of my olives, I leaned forward, losing some of my urbanity.

"Anytime you wish to partake of the frosted crab, I'll be more than happy to take you."

Her brows became a black bar.

"Are you a member?"

"No, but I do have reciprocal rights, so don't tease me."

"I wasn't. Really."

I was silent for a dogged moment.

"And, I don't go around bagging young girls like moose."

"I know."

Our manner had gone all on edge. It was a wonder dinner went as well as it did. She talked a few clever, but mostly fill-in, things. I chipped in a word now and then. Cheese and black coffee added a piquancy as we lingered at table as if it were a safety island.

"I wish I'd ordered the roe," she sighed, eyeing my empty plate.

"I would have given you half of mine."

"I know you would. You would give me all the things I don't want."

I ignored that and plunged ahead with, "There's a dance coming up—"

"Don't press."

Her face was blank. My throat plugged. I crumpled my napkin and flung it down the table saying, "Then I think we should start for the station."

She went erect in her chair. Her eyes swept the room, drifted across to the big hall, circled over the paintings and returned to me. She threw me an ugly glance and her mouth went sullen.

"In that case grab the waiter so I can pay."

Outside the night wore darker curtains.

# Chapter Fifteen

*"Why so pensive?"*

She was too young to look so knowing.

"You'll think I'm dippy," I grinned a bit wryly. "Anyway, it's a dark night and it's been a hard year so far for us both."

We were temporarily stranded in one of Baltimore's airless deli bars that one enters through the food section. The steam heat was unnerving. We walked there from the station after finding out our trains would be delayed for at least two hours. We stood at the bar. There was not a table or booth to be had. She unbuttoned the pearl buttons of her blouse and pressed her drink to that spot on her neck below her ear where I wanted to put my lips.

"Tell me," she leaned near, "and I'll buy you another drink."

"I may have seen better days, but I'm not to be had for the price of a drink."

"I'll make it two then," she teased, kittenishly.

"Hmmm. You wouldn't care to change the *quid pro quo?*"

"Such as...Oh, I see. Well, you'll have to ask my mother."

I pretended to look around the room.

"Seems she's not here. Might I ask the bartenderess?"

"Be my guest," she smirked.

"I am your guest," I reminded, and motioned to the woman dressed like a playing card. The knave.

"I have a question for you miss."

"The name's Lolly. Ask away, honey."

Lolly had a puffy, discolored face, but bright eyes.

"I want to kiss this young woman but her mother isn't here. Have I your permission?"

"Kiss away," Lolly's eyelids fluttered above the broad button of her nose, "and if you want to go for seconds, see me."

"Well? Will Lolly do?" I jested.

In the small stuffy entrance, I heard the shrill laugh and the babel of excited voices of new arrivals.

"She'll do. So tell me."

"I was thinking about milk bottles with a swelling at the neck for the cream to collect in. It must have been brought on by seeing all those cartons of milk we passed."

"That wouldn't be my interpretation."

"What would?"

"That your cultural icon hasn't been putting out, as you boys say."

My ears got hot. I finished my drink in a gulp. I should have asked what she would have said to hollyhocks and Buick Roadmasters and other good things that are going or gone. Like Gar Wood mahogany speedboats. Instead I came out with, "I could say the same about your demerara daddy."

She gave me an angry glance and I eyed her with a sort of contrite sharpness and a glow of satisfaction.

"Would you care to explain that last remark?" she demanded, drawing away from me.

Absently I lined up the ashtray with my empty glass, cigarettes and lighter. My penchant for tidying things was showing. This habit, like my shadow, has tagged along my whole life.

"I believe it's fairly obvious."

"Not to me," she snapped, her eyes stormy. "At least not the part about a dema—something daddy."

"First I'll have another drink. All right?"

"All right," she repeated.

"Thank you," I said with some agitation and waited. She pulled a cigarette from a pack in her bag. I shoved my lighter to her. Her red lips tightened. It came.

"You're welcome."

I pulled at my ear and signaled to Lolly.

"Well?"

"Demerara," I began, my voice even, "is unrefined sugar that comes from Guyana. The English have valued it since the days of the Empire. Of all the sugar imported, demerara was and is the most prized."

Her lips drew back. She cut me short.

"Then sugar daddy would have sufficed."

I eyed her for a moment.

"But certainly lack the *cachet*. Wouldn't you say?"

Her flush faded.

"So, you've heard all about Riley from Eros?"

"Not everything," I corrected. "I'm sure..."

She cut me short again.

"He's not, you know."

"He's not what?" I asked lifting my drink and looking into the glass.

"My sugar daddy. Eros wasn't either. I don't need or want a sugar daddy. If Eros told you that, he's a jerk."

She broke off and blinked.

"He didn't. He only wanted to know if I'd found out why you only seem to go for old men."

"Eros *is* a jerk," she said, irritably.

"That I couldn't say, but you love him and look at him in a way you never look at me."

Her hand slipped down from her face. She said nothing.

"Eros told me I was too young for you."

"You may be," she replied with a sort of satisfaction. "Did I tell you, you look spiffy?"

I twirled my swizzle stick.

"Spiffy?"

"There you go taking the wrong view. I would have thought you'd like the word spiffy. It's so defiantly old-fashioned. Would you have preferred nice?"

"I hate the word nice. But spiffy, well, goes with...old brass fishing reels—"

"And stamp albums," she finished.

She was young in her hardness. She sort of looked through me, as if she were seeing things a long way off. I stopped turning the ridiculous palm tree.

"Would you have told me about Riley if Eros hadn't?"

Her lashes dropped. When they lifted, her glance was inscrutable.

"Eros dislikes Riley. He refers to him as the greedy spider."

"Nice fella," I drawled, "but should I dislike him and bow out?"

She made a voice in her throat.

"If I'm going to be honest with you, then you owe me and yourself the same. Okay?"

"Okay," I grunted. "You kicked out one of my lungs the first time I saw you. You could make me die. Not kill me. Make me die. How am I doing? Is that honest enough for you? Every time I see you I want to spit on my palms, hit my fists together, and wish."

She grew less taut. Her eyes softened. There *was* something between her and me. She felt it, too. I could tell by the expression in her eyes. She looked pained. She fumbled, pushing back her hair as she fished around in a smaller version of a Gladstone bag.

"Damn, I'm out of cigarettes and I hate paying single-pack prices."

I pulled my coat from under hers to get to the extra pack in my inside glove pocket.

"Take these," I said, tackling the cellophane for her, while Lolly wiped away another summer moustache.

"Did you come into this world as prepared as a Boy Scout?"

"Don't know. Probably."

"Do you carry condoms in the pocket of that tobacco brown suede vest?"

"Four," I matched. "Two in each pocket, but what about the other two pockets? Would you care to check?"

"What would I find?"

"Oh, perhaps a sapphire ring in an old setting or a folded,

yellowing note kept near that says I love you with all the vitamins, A, B and C."

"Some other time."

"Then suppose we get back to Riley."

She began in a sweet hesitating voice.

"Riley's unrefined sugar, like me. He's sixty-four. A trial attorney. Never married. Very athletic. Lives center city. He makes a good friend but a very bad enemy and...and he knows all about you."

"And?"

She looked at me from beneath her lashes.

"Would you let anyone steal something that belonged to you?"

"Do you belong to him?"

She snubbed out her cigarette.

"I owe it to him."

"Owe?"

"He has cancer of the prostate."

"I'm sorry," I mumbled.

That did put a damper on things.

"Want another drink?" she asked, establishing eye contact.

I shook my head.

"Thanks, but I still have a little corner left."

I felt ripped to pieces. She took out her lipstick. I caught her fingers.

"Don't, I like you this way."

I decided against trying for divided sympathy. And Hector's honest, unequivocal remarks about my life expectancy. I wanted to understand her, but didn't, or the caution in her eyes.

She stared at me with distant eyes.

"Riley's a cheap Irish Mick, as they used to say, and nobody knows it better than I. But he's not a cheap one. His father was a numbers man. Riley lives well. Very well. Only the best. You'd approve of his acquired taste. He'd kill for yours and what you take for granted. Riley studies the people he copies. He almost takes them over and when he's got what he wants he drops them fast. He's dropped a lot to get where he is. It's like he flushes them away when he's done with them. The only thing important to Riley is winning."

For the first time I realized that her voice with its faltering cadence was the strongest thing in the room.

"Do you love him?"

She began with a sigh.

"Riley excites me. For all that cheapness and meanness he's the real thing. Like you."

The real thing from two different planets was what I refrained from saying.

"His hands fascinate and excite me. He could crush me in two by only using one. They're capable of killing and may have for I know he would let nothing stand between him and what he wants. And now he needs me."

I made an effort to say evenly, "Needs you? Needs you for what?"

"Riley's scared. For the first time in his life. Scared of the knife. Scared of being left impotent. Incontinent. Or both. Scared of dying. He won't have the operation and I won't leave him until he does."

With obvious relief she said, "That's it."

"I'll wait."

Her, "I didn't want you to...to like me so much, you know," came out rather sharply. "I'm making no promises." And my, "I'm not asking for any," came out rather flatly.

After a defiant moment she gave in, "I'm so damned tired."

With things left like that we left for the station to wait on the platform somewhat awkwardly, listening to the escalator creak and its side panels rattle. A frown creased her forehead.

"Answer me something," she breathed softly.

I eyed her lazily.

"If I can."

She smiled nervously.

"Why is it when I'm paying the bill and tipping generously, I'm treated as a ghost person while you're doted on? Back there at the bar that funny looking wom—"

"Her name is Lolly," I interrupted.

"How do you know that?"

"She told us. I listened."

"Well, *Lolly* was ready to run off with you."

"Perhaps," I breathed heavily, "if you showed an interest or a smile, people would respond. Interesting people are interested. Even such an enchanted nymph as you must be mortal." I drew hard on my cigarette. "You did ask."

"I'm not offended. You're probably—"

Her voice trailed away, went dead. Above the roar of trains rushing in we yelled our goodbyes. "What about coming down for a dance?" I wanted some kind of a commitment, but she slid away on, "I'll call you," and didn't turn back on boarding.

Inside my car the air was dead and hot, heavy with the sour smells of unwashed bodies and hair. Yawning people in rumpled clothes who have littered the aisle with the remains of the day, avoid eye contact as if to refute their squalor. I've only been away from my house a few hours, but already I longed to be back. Back to Danny, a fire in the fireplace and lemon verbena linen sheets. We have become a Nation of slobs. Even Wimbledon has punked out on us and the ones who should know better are no longer doing their part. I felt like the lone survivor. Like the Brass Elephant. I stared at the empty seats. One was spotted with greasy potato chip fragments. The other, strangely forlorn, with its flattened plastic straw wrappers serving as the only trace of the last occupant. Could the club car be worse? I didn't get a chance to find out. I was stopped by one whose smile was incandescent, not merely practiced. It hypnotized me. Someone who was indecently good-looking with a figure a shade too voluptuous for my taste, perhaps, but who would do any day of the week and twice on Sunday. Her inquiring glance explicitly placed me. Was I to be saved from *weltschmerz* by a woman I didn't know and probably never would?

"This is my seat," the honey voice purred. "Would you care to join me?"

With that one glance she took me in from the top of my windblown head to my plain-toe English butterscotch-grain brogues.

"I was just on my way to the club car, may I—?"

She was all white and pink and lush. Her sensuality shown like a beacon.

"Don't, it's even worse in there, if you can believe it."

Was her platinum hair dyed to match her fur coat or vice versa? The toggle on the zipper of her leather jump suit went erect everytime she exhaled.

"I'm headed for D.C.," she smiled, "what about you?"

"The same. Let me guess, you've been shopping in New York."

This time she gave me a slow smile.

"Unnh. Atlantic City."

The car swayed. I steadied myself by grabbing hold of the back of the seat. She steadied herself by putting her hand on mine.

"Did you win, lose, or break even?"

She was absolutely feminine and stronger than she looked.

"None of the above. I worked it."

She removed her hand from mine.

"Oh, you're a dancer at one of the casinos. A dream girl in those extravaganzas I've read about."

Her, "Wrong," came out like a bong. "I'm a hooker," she said without a single trace of self-consciousness. "Not that I'd ever dream of charging you. Anyone ever tell you your hair's the color of melting butter?"

I studied her with passionate curiosity. She studied the effect of what she said on me.

"Not in a long time, and not in exactly those words what with the white coming in, ah..."

"The name's Nadia."

"Well, Nadia, I was on my way to the club car—"

She tossed her coat onto the seat by the window.

"You already said that. Bring me back anything brown and I'll save you this seat."

"You do that, Nadia."

I came back with six little brown bottles and four cups. Two filled with ice. The potato chip leavings were gone.

"I'll do the honors while you get comfy," she smiled seductively.

I folded my coat and made room for it in the overhead rack, grateful that the train I'd waited over two hours for was out of Boston headed for Los Angeles for I needed a smoke. Once seated I turned my attention to her, noticing how precisely she did things.

"Do you work on the Hill?" she hostessly inquired. "A lot of my johns do. I can usually tell."

"In a way, Nadia. I live on the Hill. I'm a writer."

She stopped pouring. Her lacquered nails were longer than Calypso's in her prime.

"Like Harold Robbins?"

I laughed.

"No, more like ah—"

"I love Harold Robbins," she sounded excited and breathless. "I read *The Carpetbaggers* eighteen times. What about you?"

"Once and also *A Stone for Danny Fisher*."

"Never heard of that one. Is it new?"

"No, one of his first, I believe."

She handed me a plastic cup.

"Good as *The Carpetbaggers*?"

"Different, let's say, Nadia."

"So are you and you're sweet. I like that. Cheers. Will you light my cigarette?"

We were settling in rather well.

"I always light a lady's cigarette, Nadia."

She held her cigarette high and with style.

"Thanks. Treating a hooker like a lady and a lady like a hooker should be a rule, like knock before entering."

We looked at each other.

"Really?"

"Really."

She reached down and patted my knee.

"Yeah. Ever been with a hooker? Just female curiosity."

I took another sip of my drink.

"Only when I was in college."

"Is that when you lost your cherry?"

"Yes, I was eighteen and nervous. Not scared, mind you. She...well, she was very understanding. I saw her once after that. I was with the guy who had taken me. When he saw her coming he ran. I stayed and we chatted and I ended up taking her for an ice cream soda. She liked that. So much that she took me back to her place."

"I just bet she did. God, I would have married you, and scrubbed floors to keep you, but I beat you by seven years. I was ten. My Daddy got mine."

I swallowed hard. Very hard. Not so much shocked as saddened by the dinginess of her beginnings.

She eyed me imperturbably and inhaled almost hungrily.

"You get over it. So you don't have to say anything."

"How?"

"By leaving home when I was twelve."

"Twelve!" I repeated.

She brushed aside my reaction and carefully, as if it were the most important act in the world, put out her cigarette. Then raised her great luminous eyes to mine.

"Yep. Twelve. It was Mother's Day. We were at church. Daddy was strict about church. We never missed a Sunday. I told Mama I had to go pee and crawled over Wesley."

"Wesley?"

The long fingers drummed on the fold down tray.

"My brother. He's older by three years and was hitting two hundred pounds then."

"I see."

I didn't.

"And I did have a pee. So it wasn't like I lied to Mama. Only after the pee I walked out to the highway to hitch my way to California. Hollywood, California. The third car stopped, just like that."

"You must have been very mature for twelve," was the best I could muster.

"Mature hell! I looked and was a little girl. You wouldn't

believe the perverts out there waiting to fuck a little girl. Listen, the hair's natural. I swear to God and it matches with you know what. Just try to find a rusty root, but these hot tits and ass are man made. I was flat as a pancake front and back. I could have stayed twelve forever. The problem was I kept growing. I was five foot nine when my pimp fixed me up with a Beverly Hills plastic surgeon. He would do the job for free provided he got drop in privileges. Four years of drop ins. He got his money's worth. He even had me drop by the hospital when he had an appendectomy."

When she paused to refill her cup I passed her mine.

"Those years of church-going stood me good, 'cause God's been with me all the way. My pimp had class. He treated me like his daughter. Never laid a finger on me. Only the best and the safest johns for me. He wanted to put a contract out on Daddy. When I decided to leave California because of all the freaks and branch out on my own it was with his blessings. It was only after Daddy got run over by the tractor that I went back to see Mama and Wesley. I used to call Mama when I knew Daddy was out in the field. Do you know the son of a bitch had a full military funeral with honors? He was a sergeant in the Air Force when he met Mama, stationed outside of Heidelberg, and lied to her about the big time life she would have married to him. Big time, my foot. The first thing I had Mama do was sell that damn farm. She did, and bought herself the cutest little place in town for her and Wesley, and I bought them a building at the busiest intersection for a restaurant. Mama always loved cookin' and bakin' and Wesley...well, Wesley always loved eatin'. He's a mama's boy which is kinda good for he'll never leave Mama. He's learned to cook like Mama, too, and the business is booming what with the seal of approval from the truckers."

She added some ice to her cup, looking at me, but I said nothing. Only watched as she held up the cup with a little admiration.

"I can live anywhere and have. So can anyone else."

Not everyone I thought, admiring her greatly.

"I've done all right. I have a condo and own a BMW. Pay

no taxes. Have a mutual fund for retirement and a stock broker who admires *my* business savvy. The looks won't hold forever. I may look twenty, but I'm pushing thirty-one. The ingenue days are winding down and when they do I'll be ready. I'm planning on opening family-oriented laundromats in Arkansas. That way I can be near Mama and Wesley. I plan on putting in large-screen televisions, free coffee and sodas and a room for kids filled with nothing but giant multi-colored sponge balls. I saw a room like that once in a nursery owned by a trick of mine. I can't have kids. Daddy was kinda big and rough, but I've had no diseases. Not even the clap."

"Where are Mama and Wesley?" I asked, not wanting here anymore about diseases.

"Living in a little town you never would have heard of," she laughed, good naturedly, "Ferriday—."

"Not Ferriday, Louisiana?"

"You know the place!"

"I wasn't always old, Nadia. Jerry Lee Lewis was from Ferriday."

"*Goodness, Gracious, Great Balls of Fire,*" she sang out.

"*A Whole Lot of Shakin' Going On,*" roared I.

"Yeah, and *Breathless.* They sure as hell were great songs."

"They sure as hell were. What's your real name, Nadia?"

"How do you know Nadia isn't?"

"'Cause no one from Ferriday, Louisiana, was ever named Nadia."

"You're right. It's Eldyne. Eldyne Schlosser. And you're a handsome guy. Stop thinking of yourself as old."

"Nadia, I am old. I was born the year meat rationing ended in the United States. That was in nineteen forty-four."

"We once had meat rationing?" she asked, not believing.

"Only during World War II."

"Well, that's still not very old. Will you tell me your name?"

I told her.

"That's a nice name."

"Thank you."

"Now, will you tell me about your books?"

A freight train going in the opposite direction rumbled past our window. I made a fresh drink, pouring the last of the ice into my cup. Nadia was the kind of audience a writer craves. She listened. She made observing comments. She had read one of my books. She gave me a lift, as well as offering to give me one to the house. She did own a BMW. And as to what I was doing in Baltimore, she didn't ask.

We parked in front of what is mine. As always I am comforted and strengthened by the gentle peace of the old bricks, the tactile pleasures derived from inside, and Danny. Most of all, Danny. At heart, I dislike ever leaving its walls.

"This is just the kind of house I pictured you living in," she said, reluctantly turning back to me.

I wondered why the downstairs lights were on at this time of night.

"Did you?" I smiled, forgetting about the lights.

"Yes, I did. Say, am I going to end up in one of your books?"

"Would you like that, Eldyne Schlosser?"

"Better than anything," she giggled.

"I'll make no promises, Nadia, but writers do use everything and you are a charming as well as a remarkable character. By the way, Nadia suits you. It's the name for a princess. A Russian princess."

"I don't kiss johns, but you're no john. Will you kiss me? Kiss me and tell me I'm nice? Nicer than any— "

I tilted up her chin, kissed her and looked into her eyes. She had closed them, but I told her the truth.

"You're nicer than anybody, Nadia. The nicest girl I ever met and if I weren't— "

"Married and in love with someone else," she finished.

I grunted a reluctant confirmation.

She took my hand and pressed it to her cheek. In the moonlight I saw her frown. "Oh, you've gone and lost the stone in your ring."

"There was no stone to lose, Nadia. The engraving on the ring is recessed."

"So it is. Silly me. The moon tonight almost resembles what we call harvest moons back home. Would you want me as a virgin?"

Caught in indecision, I felt like a small boy ready to kick his heels against a curb.

"They're both lucky," she sighed, releasing my hand, "but don't let the one you think you're in love with ruin things for you. You're a good man. A proper gentleman."

That made me cough.

"Nadia, I don't have a card on me. but I'm in the telephone book. Send me your mother's address. Who knows, you may end up in a book. Oh, and Nadia, I thank you, more than you'll ever know, for the honor. I'm *Breathless*."

# Chapter Sixteen

*Standing on the stoop, Danny's words burned into my brain.* "Your agent died in her chicken salad at *21*. Sasha wants you to—." Backlighted as she was by the branched gasolier, Danny resembled nothing less than a vengeful Brunhilde. I listened, hoping I'd heard wrong. "—you're to be a pallbearer. I told Sasha you were away."

"Away!" I shouted, "I was in Baltimore."

Danny shot me a peculiar glance and in a tight voice repeated, "Yes, away. Away with what's her name? 'Little Miss Philly.'"

I felt embarrassed at being read like a menu. I coughed and Danny went off, mumbling like an outraged bee, but not before solicitously brushing a speck of something from my shoulder.

'Burnsie's' unexpected demise left me incapacitated with feelings of vulnerability. I smoked endlessly before abandoning my bed to wander silently around the house and then out onto the gallery where moonlight filtered through the trumpet vines to make patterns of shade and silver at my feet. Edith Burns, 'Burnsie,' discovered me. Made me. Understood my droll, quirky paragraphs. The character, place and mood of manners and morals of White Anglo-Saxon Protestants receding in a new and difficult world. "The game of life is won by inches," and Burnsie won by being a little older, a little faster, and a little smarter than those she mother-cubbed to success. She knew that while Ascot may be "U," it was the Henley Royal Regatta that was *England*. She'd once lashed out at a reviewer who'd lambasted me for being too far removed from real life with, "So what, the author is who he is, and knows who he is. Would you prefer he be from a reservation and write dross?" Our contract had been a handshake. Had she read my last chapter? I'd find out in the morning, and not from someone wearing pearls smelling of smoke.

When Amanda breezed into my study, cool and trig, it was about nine-thirty. Her brief occasional visits drench me in her warmth and always take me by surprise. No one answered at Number One, Fifth Avenue. Never had not some voice, familiar or unfamiliar, failed to eventually pick up at the cavernous co-op at Washington Square.

"How come no pages? How come no calls? How come so glum?" Amanda quizzed, giving me a long-distance look. *And*, how come the robe and slippers. I've never seen you not dressed. You know, you look kinda cute in jammies with your hair uncombed. You should shave though. White stubble is a real turnoff."

I listened listlessly, while taking in the silky Indian vest burnished with copper embroidery being worn with pale lemon Oxford cords, a silk D'Artagnan blouse and her signature five-inch patent leather heels. The Louise Brook hair has never been blacker or brighter, but her face appeared drawn.

"You're not looking so perky yourself, Amanda," I said sounding a bit fractious.

"We're talking about you, honey," she reminded, laying down her keyring with its ornamental buffalo nickel the size of a cow pie. How many years had the key to the front door been interspersed with the keys to her life?

"You go first, friend," I offered, fighting my way to change the subject.

"Well, I'm in love," she announced with a svelte spin.

"Love will do it every time," I frowned, staring past her.

"Tell me about it, honey. Love's like believing you can peel onions without tears."

Out of the mouths of models.

"Amanda?" I asked with a thin smile, "Do I have your permission to use that in a book?"

"It's yours," she humored.

"I will, and it goes without saying I wish you well."

"Wish me over it, honey."

"Why?" I stirred.

"Because I know what would happen if I gave in to my feelings. Feelings! Why kid myself and you. It's lust. Pure unadulterated lust."

"Does the object of this desire know?"

"Oh, he knows all right. That's why I won't go out with him. That's why no more modeling for this jazz baby until it passes."

"What does that have to—?"

"Everything, my man. He's this season's hot photographer. He calls the shots. If I went out with him, he'd eat me alive and leave my carcass thrown on the side of some road."

I straightened up saying, "You certainly know yourself, Amanda."

"I learned the hard way. You may not believe this, but it's been six years. I thought I was over all that, but I go to type and, wham, I was about to go again."

Amanda's spunky and fey in equal parts. My disembodied voice inquired, "Have you considered having that most treasured pearl bronzed?"

"Often," she choked, "but not anymore. I'm taking your advice. I'm going to become a candy striper and, hopefully, marry a doctor."

I pulled myself out of myself.

"Let's drink to that, and to the doctor who'll carry you over a threshold. I'd stop writing if I could get you settled."

The glare in her green eyes was short-lived and she drawled with amiable reproach, "You're blinkeyed if you think I've stuck with you for the money."

A silence fell.

"If I appear blinkeyed, Amanda, its because my agent died."

"Holy shit!" she said in a new tone of voice.

"Holy shit is right. Want a drink?"

"Nah. It's too early. Too early for us both."

I switched off the desk lamp.

"Well, at least sit down. I'm getting a crick in my neck, just like I did when I first saw the Eiffel Tower."

She poured herself into the curved-back rosewood chair and we sank into a whisper.

"When did she die?" she asked, lighting a Virginia Slim.

"Yesterday, according to Danny, while having lunch at *21*."

Amanda's beautiful, long-eyelashed face tipped itself back. She stretched out those long legs, crossed her slim ankles, and made a smoke ring.

"What killed her?"

"Don't know. Danny took the call. She said Burnsie just up and died in her chicken salad."

"Must have been a hell of a wishbone," Amanda mused. "Her family could probably sue."

"Her clients were her family. Burnsie was a spinster."

"Get you! Am I a spinster?"

"Don't fish, Amanda. You know what I mean. Burnsie was somewhere in her seventies."

"What's my man going to do?"

"I'm to be a pallbearer. After that I don't know. I'm trying to find out if she had comments on that last chapter."

"Stop worrying, I read everything you write. This is your best book."

This time my confidence stirred.

"Thanks. Have something to eat." I pushed the tray in need of plating toward her. "You always liked Danny's quince jelly."

"I certainly do, and this is the only place in town to get it."

She spread a generous helping on a biscuit.

"You're not eating?"

"Never do this early, and I couldn't eat today if I did. This is Danny's idea of elevenses. That's why the extra allotment of sugar cookies and the thermos of pure Darjeeling tea for my agitated nerves. Here, I'll go rinse my cup for you."

"Pour. It's not as if it's your toothbrush. What about those pages I returned?"

I burned them, Amanda. "I must have written them under a misbegotten fool moon."

"You're right about that, honey."

Amanda and I have a healthy respect for each other.

"So where do you go from here?"

The window pane was shining with running rain.

"I don't know," I admitted with a worried sigh, "I'm at a career crisis."

"Fiddlesticks," she cried, holding out her cup for more tea.

"But, I am Amanda. It seems my earlier works were preferred for their spirit of youth. Now those with liberal principles are deeming me out of fashion for seeing the end coming. I'm allergic to failure, being accustomed to matters as they were, so I know of no immunity for it." I paused to put out a cigarette and started another. "And I've gotten myself in an increasingly uncomfortable relationship by—"

"Falling in love," Amanda finished. "Really in love."

"It shows?"

"Only a lot. Tell me about her." She ran the toe of her shoe against my calf. "Let's see if mama can make it better."

"You always had a quick discerning mind, Amanda."

"It doesn't take a quick mind to discern when a person's hyper and happy. And it's been a long time since the heavy-duty, high-maintenance Calypso Fox, Miss Fox to me, to paraphrase Cole Porter, made you feel that way."

The whine of a police siren carried clearly across the square. This morning, the square where children laze with bare feet in summer, is bare and sodden.

"Talk to mama," she nudged again.

"Danny loathes her."

"That's understandable," she commented, her eyes deceptively blank.

"Whatever for?"

Amanda looked at me silently for a few seconds, and I saw conflicting emotions chase each other across her face. Then with studied control, she answered, "One thing at a time. Start at the beginning. You went to Philadelphia in November. You weren't in love when you left, so that had to be when you met her."

My blankly regarding the terra-cotta freckles across the bridge of her nose caused her to become exasperated.

"If you remember, you called me the next evening ebullient beyond belief. Talk."

Clearing my throat, I began, "Pass me that cup. You won't—"

"Nothing can or does surprise me. So start."

So I did, and when I finished, Amanda lit another cigarette, leaned back and puffed coolly.

"Baby, all I can say is you're living a new book. So start writing it all down and then kiss her off. She's a trip not worth taking."

"Nothing else, Amanda?"

"Only this, you can't make love happen. It's like a kind of gift. Like faith. So give up the *gauche*. She's impinged on your life long enough. You're not the gloomy type by nature, and she's cataclysmic. I'll leave you to think about that. Gotta go." She leaned forward and tapped me on the chin, "You'll be all right. Trust mama."

"Amanda, volunteer at Sibley. There's a Doctor Ferguson, first name Guy. You'd like him. Trust me."

"I'm out of here! Get cleaned up. You'd feel better."

"Where's your coat?"

"Cape," she corrected. "It's downstairs."

"'The Little Red Riding Hood' one?"

"Yeah. The one that brings out the wolf in you."

I rose to that by giving her a long wailing cry.

Amanda shook her head.

"I'll check on you this evening. Bye."

"Bye."

Some of my old confidence edged back, watching her leave. For the first time I speculated on what our relationship would be under normal conditions, whatever normal is, and decided to leave it alone and instead do as she said. I was rubbing my head with a towel when the telephone rang, and I lunged for the receiver like a drowning man.

"Sasha! I've been trying to reach you for—." Sasha? Who is this? Eros! Oh, sorry, Eros. Its just...well, I thought it was my agent's secretary, Sasha. No, my book hasn't sold. My agent died yesterday. Yes, that's right. Eros, its a long story. I can hardly hear you. From where are you calling? The *Casa* what? The *Casa Bobo*? No? Where? The *Casa Poo-Poo*? "You're having a crap as we speak? No, I don't keep a phone in the lavatory. I'd be afraid of being electrocuted. It's cordless. Well, I suppose so, but I prefer black rotary and, well, I was never one to linger. You're fading, Eros. Oh, you're flushing." I stopped listening until I heard him say "Baltimore." "What about Baltimore, Eros? Oh, no, I cannot meet you, I'll be leaving for New York. I'm to be a pallbearer. Yes, I suppose medical conventions are lonely affairs. How's your wife? Our mutual friend told me. When? In passing. Then why not bring your daughter? Couldn't you prescribe Dramamine for the night cruise down the Chesapeake? She might meet a—. Nothing, Eros. Skip it. Yes, as a matter of fact, I have. Yesterday, in Baltimore. Nothing's changed. She leaves me lovesick and under ether. I spend half my nights trying to figure her out. You too, Eros, I'm flattered that you thought of me first."

Our brief colloquy was followed by a dead sound. I moved on to the study to finish off the Darjeeling. The champagne of teas was flat. I set the cup down with a bang and dialed Burnsie's number. Sasha picked up and immediately burst into tears.

"Do stop sniffling, Sasha, you know you'll dehydrate. Well, you can at least try. How do you think I feel? The magnitude of the pain. You at least—. Everything was to go to you unless she changed her will. I didn't think so. So you can at least retire.

I on the other hand, well that can wait. Yes, of course, I'll be a pallbearer. When? At eleven. Who else? That is an august group. I feel like wearing a black arm band, but instead I'll wear my black velvet-collared herringbone. The Fifth Avenue Presbyterian Church? I thought as much. She left the choir ten thousand dollars! Well, she did love choir boys. Would you make me a reservation at New York Athletic? Thank you, but I wouldn't feel comfortable alone in that draughty apartment. Well, if you're going to be moving in. Yes, why waste good money. Especially mine. Ah, Sasha, what exactly—? It was a wishbone. Good God!"

The trip up was Kafkaesque. I sat stiff and straight trying to shut out the uncivilized decibel level of those around me and was as vulnerable to this as I was to what lay ahead. The situation was not unlike suddenly becoming an orphan, except I wasn't as concerned about finding a parent as I was another agent the likes of Burnsie, and that wasn't going to be possible. At times, the train crawled and when it did, the engine died away and we came to bumping standstills. So, I was late for Burnsie's funeral, but so was the hearse from Frank E. Campbell. How such a little woman could weigh so much staggered me. Was Burnsie taking her books with her? Or was I getting older by the minute? God knows. At Brooklyn's Holy Cross Cemetery, that lean-and-hungry-for-more-success-twenty-six-year-old author of quadruple incest and murder in Appalachia, currently enjoying an unprecedented eighty-two week run on the *New York Times* Best Seller List, started off by treating me as if I were some in-decline Henry James. So solicitous was he that later, at The Colony, he stopped swigging down his beer from a bottle long enough to offer to find me a chair while offhandedly asking if I were still writing. I snarled, too loudly, "That I was and that the doorknocker was still on the front door." After that, I drank too many blood-orange screwdrivers and went off to sulk in the Elsie de Wolfe room by a blue-green crackle fire that was wilting the white cabbage roses in a silver bowl. The prick! Does he drink his beer from a bottle in front of his father? And, if he doesn't remove his worn-backwards New York Yankees baseball hat as a pallbearer, when does he? Perhaps the time had come for me to read Burton's *Anatomy of Melancholy*. The next morning my bad foot was goutish. I had to use my return ticket for a shoehorn. When I found Sasha in the dining room she was counting teaspoons, with her eyes shut and her face slack in what amounted to unnatural orgasmic ecstasy.

"Your tears dry quickly, Sasha."

"What?" she jumped, losing count.

"Burnsie, had she comments on my last chapter?"

"What?"

"May I see Burnsie's comments? What's going on with Random House?"

"I—I don't know."

Her arms attempted to draw the table full of silver to her.

"You'll have to talk with Pauli Arn—"

"That Philistine! Why must I speak to him?"

"I've sold him the agency. That's why. He'll carry you—"

"Carry me! A Susie Wong has more taste."

"Suit yourself. Mr. Arnson— Pauli thought you might become rediscovered."

Sasha's statement carried like an arctic slap of wind.

"Sasha!"

I'd never noticed how much her hatchet face resembled Margot Asquith.

"Well, it's true. Pauli's not interested in past success. Today is what counts. Like that boy to whom you were so insulting, who was only trying to be nice."

"Since when is condescending nice? The kid's an out-and-out shit. Hell, he treated me like an old stuffed sofa."

"Suit yourself," she repeated, starting to recount the silver. From the hall, I shouted that I was taking the picture of Burnsie and me at the Waldorf the night I'd won the—. I'm as good as I ever was. Better even. Pauli Arnson can go—. "Take any of them. Only leave the frames."

I slid the picture into my leather overnight "Doctor's" bag and walked out. At Penn Station, I turned in my ticket and took a taxi to Idlewild. For the first time in my life, I took the shuttle back to Washington. Minutes don't really count when one takes the long view. No desk therapy awaited me. Only Danny, same as it ever was it seemed, and Danny was commanding my attention with her sense and sensibility when the telephone interrupted us. She took the call, went stiff, then handed the receiver to me.

"'Little Miss Philly,'" she announced formally and, not leaving, frankly listened.

"Your boss servant doesn't like me," my caller opened.

"I think you have an imagination problem."

"I don't think so. Is she nearby?"

"Yes, as a matter of fact."

"Eros told me your agent died."

"Unfortunately so. I only returned this morning from her funeral. I'm at an impasse, though Danny won't have me saying it."

"What are you going to do?"

"Trust in the Lord. Something will turn up."

"It certainly will," Danny agreed with dogmatic determination, while the one on the other end asked if I would still like for her to come down for the dance?

"More than anything."

"What about her?"

"Who?"

"Danny."

"I can handle that."

"I thought she handled you."

"You thought wrong."

"Then, what about Calypso?"

"Calypso's away in Dallas at a Golden Door."

"Houston," Danny wedged in.

"What's a Golden Door?"

"A kind of spa that spoils the inner child in us in a Zen-like atmosphere of pampering."

"Calypso Fox has no inner self, that's her biggest problem," Danny wedged in again, "much as I am beginning to kinda like her. She's an acquired taste, and for what she's paying that place she could have had a neck lift, which is what she needs, and which is what I told her."

I stared at Danny, but her eyes never backed down. She departed the study in a huff, banging the door behind her to keep in the heat.

"What was that?"

"Danny on her way out."

"Is she that mad about my calling you?"

"Suffice it to say that Danny's mad. We'll have the house to ourselves by the way. Danny will be away at a wedding. Her niece, the one who is a special agent, is marrying a stockbroker."

"Strange combination."

"Safe combination, I'd say. She's a top marksman and was first in her class at the FBI Academy. The woman can assemble and load a machine gun in ninety seconds."

"Where did they meet?"

"Skeet shooting."

"Are you all right?"

"I am now."

"There's a three-thirty train that will put me in at five-thirty. Will you meet me?"

"Listen to my heart."

"I'll see you next Friday then."

"Thank you."

"For what?"

"For caring enough to call."

Like a creeping cloud, Sasha's words hung at the back of my mind. Day went into night. Night went into day. Each endless and empty. What saved me was planning for our weekend. Together and alone, once the dance was behind us. Nothing would be left to chance. I planned everything down to asking Caroline at Tune-Inn to save four fresh crab cakes, as well as to remind her of my guest's name and to be especially cordial to her. I invited friends to come early for drinks before the dance at ten and cleaned off two bottles of cider brought up from the root cellar to do their quiet magic by a fire. By my calculations, the cider was older than our combined ages. And when I heard the phone, I opened with, "I knew that would be you."

"Now how would you know that?" she mocked.

"Don't know, but I knew. Great minds, I guess."

"Perhaps, but I called because—"

I felt dead.

"You're not coming!"

"Of course, I'm coming, but I'll need to get back Saturday morning."

"Saturday!"

"Yes, I'm free at last. Free of all of them. I've sold my shares in the company. But, instead of taking a lump sum, I'll continue to draw a weekly salary until the amount is paid off. I've just signed the papers. I want to clean out my things and try to get settled in at Andrea's. I have three interviews lined up for Monday. Are you going to be disappointed?"

"Yes, why lie, but I'm delighted that you're out of there. That drive of yours is one of the things I admire most about you. Tell you what. I declined the Lammers' party. I'll accept and we'll go back together. Why not come with—"

"Not likely."

"Why? Do you know the Lammers'?"

"If they're the ones who live in *Maro Manor* out in Villanova, I do. Well, I know one of their daughters anyway. Alexandra. Her mother rides? Right?"

"Suzanne hunts on Tuesdays and Thursdays in season."

"Thought so, and they are the people you would know."

I let that pass.

"See you Friday."

"Wait! What train are you taking back?"

"I hadn't thought about it. Why?"

"I'll need to order my tickets."

"Order your tickets?"

"Yes."

"You don't buy your tickets at the station?"

"And stand in line? No, I call my travel agent. She, Patricia, sends them over by messenger."

"You have life down to a science."

"I try. Why make things hard?"

The girl whose train I met, and took to Tune-Inn for crab cakes and Caroline's cordiality, didn't look like a bright young businesswoman. Her skin was clear and fresh and scrubbed and totally unresponsive to emotions below the surface. I am happy, but I feel like crying, and I have gone to heaven only to become tongue-tied and she tight-lipped with her compliments. Even her comment on the fence, as the cab pulled up to the house was double-edged. Mine was, "I'm surprised you noticed. Trap and—"

"Who's Trap?"

"Trap is my yardman," I explained. "You'll meet him tonight. I asked him to come in to do drinks and clean up. He and Danny had Libby, Libby Bryant, gold leaf the finials for my Christmas present. Libby's an art restorer. She's worked on most everything inside. Danny overheard Libby telling me about a fence she was doing for a hotel in Alexandria."

"How many serfs have you?" was the comment I did not let pass.

"None, but I do have friends who...who appreciate me, and take me as I am."

Notwithstanding, I forgot her verbal chaffing when I caught her reflection in my bedroom looking glass, wearing a tawny port velvet gown designed by someone who really loved women, judging by the way it followed her body's curves and the scooped-out neckline. I swallowed hard, "That dress should only be worn in candlelight," and finished tying my tie.

"Father can't tie black tie, much less white pique. I've never known a man that could. George tried and gave up."

"What about Riley? Sorry about that."

"It's all right. Riley can't tie and doesn't own. Did I mention that Riley's decided he wants to live? He was operated on this morning."

My world went swinging around. I spilled cider, ignored it, and gulped down the rest.

"How's he doing?" I asked woodenly. She shrugged. The

long and heavy drop earrings danced. I watched eyes I could not read. Eyes devoid of devilment. Eyes that would only know more. In a complacent voice she said, "No idea. They hadn't finished with him when I left. I'll check tomorrow."

The doorknocker sounded twice. I put on my tailcoat and tucked my white kid gloves into my breast pocket, fingers out.

"Shall we go down and greet our first quests?"

# Chapter Seventeen

*Devron's smooth rhythms floated in the air from the second floor* and out over Dupont Circle, as the heavy old doors were swung wide. That she was here gave everything a false dreamlike security. Reception rooms were swarming, bursting with the crowd. The world is a brass band and she is doing the thing so well. I slipped my hand through her arm and maneuvered her up the wide curving stairway full of handsome people laughing and calling out and bypassed the receiving line wreathed in regulation smiles. I was hungry for absolute pleasure before the world ends. Centered in the gilded cove ceiling of the baroque ballroom, the bronze chandelier blazed out with its one hundred and one lights. The roar of the room was high. Holding her close, a strand of her hair brushed for an instant against my cheek, and I felt warmed clear down to the soles of my patent leather shoes. But, for whatever reason, she didn't look as happy as I expected.

"Something wrong?"

"Kinda."

"What?"

"I don't dance."

"Don't or won't?"

"Don't. I don't know how."

"You're being coy? Right?"

"Wrong."

There was nothing else I could think of to say to that. My arms tightened round her. "Then fake it. I'll lead. You follow." She couldn't, and I let myself forget how well Calypso and I dance and that my new partner couldn't. In the whirl of bright gowns and black coats, the awful Grahams circled like vultures ready to go to the whispering galleries with any pickings. I wanted to stick my tongue out at them and would have had Henry Mackall not cut in before I could come to a standstill.

"I think they can manage introductions," Henry's golden haired wife laughed.

"I suppose, Margaret," I said, kissing her hand and clicking my heels formally for fun. Devron waved his men into a romantic strain and his fingers swept over the keys. "Drink or dance?"

"Dance, what do you think? How often do I have the opportunity when Calypso instantly languishes like Proust's Duchesse de Guermantes at sightings of any reasonably attractive woman."

"You're more than reasonably attractive, Margaret."

"You didn't have to say that."

"I know. That's why I said it."

"I'd almost forgotten what it was like to dance with you. And speaking of Calypso—"

"Were we?"

"I was anyway. Where is she?"

"Dallas. Houston. I forget."

"Not drying out again, surely?"

"No, we no longer have that problem, Margaret. Calypso's gone to one of those spas that pampers you to death while helping you find the inner self."

"Don't make me laugh. Are you sure she's not having a face lift?"

"That's what Danny told her she should be having for what she's paying. Actually, it was a neck lift."

"Knowing Danny, I'm sure she did. Who is that divine child with two left feet dancing with Henry?"

"A daughter of friends."

"I'm glad I don't have friends with daughters who look like that. Look at Henry. Well, it serves him right. She has absolutely no sense of rhythm. Where is she from?"

"Philadelphia."

"Philadelphia's big."

"Chestnut Hill."

"Do I know them?"

"Probably."

Sweet Jesus! The snap on my right glove popped open. Fool that I am, I'd never bothered to find out their Christian names.

"I think we had best go rescue Henry. Be kind."

"I'm always kind."

Margaret and Henry didn't know her family. When they asked where she was staying, a hasty glance was cast my way. I dabbed at my forehead. Henry looked past my shoulder. Margaret laughed, but her eyes were intelligent. Thinking quickly, I said, "She knows Nancy."

"I actually don't know her, but I've seen her play at Brandywine several times."

To that I added, "Where is the lively Nancy, Margaret? I haven't seen her."

"Argentina."

"With her ponies?"

"All six. I told Nancy not to take her ponies to a country that was so chauvinistic."

"Are they?" I managed, for my guest was not troubling herself to talk.

"Are they! They're simply prehistoric. The last of the Latin Lovers. Would your young friend enjoy going to the club tomorrow afternoon to see a match?"

"She's leaving in the morning, Margaret."

Henry's mouth split into the family grin. He rubbed his ear doubtfully. "Isn't that our song, Margaret?"

"Henry, you say every song is our song."

"I do," his Tidewater voice agreed, "and right now it happens to be *It Had to be You*."

"Bye," Margaret waved hurriedly. "Call us when Calypso returns."

"Well," I winked when they had gone, "we're back where we started." I reached out for her and she stepped back, "Once should be enough for even the bravest heart, I should think."

"Not with you," I whispered, pressing my mouth into her hair. "Not when you're so lovely."

She stole me a glance. "It's all so socially interchangeable."

"What?"

"Your world, their world," she said a mite too chiding, I felt. "And it's all connected by sleepy pleasantries."

"Yes, well," I said under my breath, whirling her around the mirrored walls, "and some would say pearls are fancy oyster grit."

"Showing off?"

"A little."

"Well, stop. You'll make me sick."

"Not if you look into my eyes and stay fixed there. Look at me, dammit."

I wanted to conquer her. I wanted her to give up.

"No, please."

I spun her faster. Everything blurred 'round us.

"Please. Please stop."

"Say uncle."

She was panting.

"Say it."

"Uncle."

I stopped.

"Thank you," she said not looking at me.

I felt hot.

"You're welcome."

"Who's the man waving to us? The one who looks like he was born in a tuxedo?"

"Devron. Howard Devron. Come on, I'll introduce you."

"Nothing's wrong with Calypso, is there?" Howard asked, rising from his bench. "She hasn't had a—?"

"Absolutely nothing, Howard," I boomed false heartily. "Calypso's away having a little R&R before getting ready for her Bergdorf showing and this young beauty, a daughter of friends in Philadelphia, has saved me from coming stag by happening to be in town."

He smiled brightly both hands out to her. "Would you 'save' me from a lonely widowerhood, if there is such a word?"

"Could I think about it?" she said swiftly.

"I'm only joking. Marion could never be replaced. That's why I sold our place on Lake Chapala in Mexico and came out of retirement. Do you know Calypso Fox?"

"Only by reputation."

"Well, let me tell you. She's magical. Supreme. Not Brenda. Not Hope. Not CZ's daughter came close. I've played for them all. I should write a book. I've been approached. It's a dying world. Dead, really. Nevertheless, I'm grateful for our having had sons. Not all girls can handle too much, too soon. Didn't somebody use that as a title?"

"Diana Barrymore, Howard."

"What a memory this guy has," he said, swallowing some water the way he always does before singing. "Be sure to tell Calypso my first song was her favorite."

"Which is?" my young guest asked, picking listlessly at a palm frond.

"A little ditty I wrote called, *Dreams Will Come True Again, For Everything Old Is New Again.*"

"*I'm* not, Howard."

"You're a squirt, pal."

He picked up his microphone and the music beat like a pulse in my blood.

"Long Island/Jazz Age parties/Waiter bring us two more Barcardis/Dreams will come true again/For everything old is new again/Put on your top hat/Your white tie and tails/Let's go backward to Woolworth sales/Leave Greta Garbo alone/Be a movie star on your own/Don't throw the past away/You may need it some rainy day/Dreams will come true again/For everything old is new again."

She let herself go against me for a moment. I tucked her arm into mine, "How about a drink?" "I thought you'd never ask, suh." My eyebrows raised in amusement. "Demure doesn't suit you," and we went to join the others. That she was clubfooted on a dance floor didn't deter the unknowing. Off she went and back she came. Two red-headed young men rushed over shoulder to shoulder, one asked her for the samba and the other the rumba. I tossed down a whisky and leaned back in a tapestry-covered chair, chatting, but mostly listening to subdued ripples of conversation proud that my charge was holding her own. On going down to supper, she breathed in my ear, "Won't it ever be done?" "Soon," I replied. But not soon enough. Daylight was coming thinly in when maids, in ruffled half-aprons, began collecting glasses, emptying ashtrays and lowering lights.

In the taxi she appeared bored with no soft or nasal Southern voices flowing over us. "Tell me something," she snapped, if snapping can be done in a whisper. The fat little driver with the corrugated brows cocked his ears. He almost looked naked without the genial smile.

"Yes."

"What's exactly is Calypso Fox's problem?" She almost caressed the words.

I felt uneasy, "What do you mean?"

"All those veiled inquiries regarding her health. *Why* is she in Texas?"

"You already know why."

I asked the driver if I could smoke. I could as long as I rolled down the window on the dusky bloom of morning.

"Beyond that."

I coughed at my disloyalty, let go of her soft palm and pulled away from the scent of jasmine that made my liver quiver.

"Calypso had nothing to fall back on when her fame passed. The 'lay-me-down-and-die-sugar-blues' she called it when her life went from fireworks to hysteria. A typical American climax in many ways."

"Can't you just say she went nuts?" she admonished in a voice inclined to fight.

I colored up.

"Not really."

"What then, a lush?"

Harsh are the young.

"Calypso never drank during meals, only in between to chase away the shadows on the wall. But, yes, she did drink to escape the demons. *Drank* to be more precise. For she doesn't anymore."

"So what's with Bergdorf's and this showing? Is Calypso coming back as a model for the older woman?"

"Calypso? Good Lord, she's never done an honest days work until now. No, when Calypso was...was away...away in Stockbridge—"

"Stockbridge?"

"Stockbridge, Massachusetts, the ah...her doctor enrolled her in an arts and craft class and...and, as she would tell you, she found God in a glue gun. Don't laugh. It was there that her latent artistic streak erupted, and its been spewing ever since. That silver champagne cooler atop the highboy in my—"

"She did that!"

"It was one of her first things after she was...after she returned. Then came presents for friends. The word spread. Little Caledonia, a toney shop in Georgetown, now carries her things. But, it was after the Junior League Christmas show that Bergdorf's signed her."

"I take it, her things aren't cheap?"

Did I detect the yowl of a cat ready to spit?

"Calypso was never cheap."

"And each has his own cross to bear, doesn't one?"

That put me at a loss. We said no more. It was as if she'd flung herself out of the cab. I fitted the key in the door and stood aside for her. While I went to hang my coat, she went on up to the night nursery, for she had not wished to stay in the room Ursula and I had shared. The kiss I forced out of her was so light and perfunctory that it made me angry. She need not have done it at all, I wanted to say, and it was definitely not worth climbing the steep narrow stairs for. I felt abysmally tired and indifferent. Sulkily, her eye on the door, as if she had already locked it, she said, "Let's stick to our boundaries." It was like a nightmare of something which might have been wonderful and now was far off and tasteless. A short silence fell, broken by my voice. "There's a 10:05 train that will put us in at 12:10. Bud is meeting me. Does that get you in too late? We can drop you at your new place." For a moment I thought she looked surprised, even a little relieved, then the expression vanished and the set expression on her face was answer enough. "No, it wouldn't be too late," she answered, turning off the nightlight in Ludwig's folly. This left me to shut what I'd hoped to be an open door.

My neck felt like a corkscrew and I was red-eyed when I went down the backstairs to scrounge up something in the kitchen. The all-knowing Danny had left me to fend on my own. And, on my own, I would starve, for the best I can manage is Bananas Foster and strong black coffee which, in this case, was enough for breakfast. Their combined aromas brought her down without my having to bother to go up to knock.

"Organized as always," she opened offhandedly, entering the kitchen from the garden room.

I steadied my breath, "Am I?"

"You're dressed, aren't you. I passed your bags in the hall. You're packed and ready. The table's set and a fire's going."

"Well," I said a little too loudly, "I came by it naturally, one could say. What about you? Aren't you set to leave?"

"Just about. What smells so good besides the coffee?"

"Bananas Foster."

She was farther away than the stars, and I was so very conscious of having made a fool of myself.

"I'm impressed."

"No need to be. It's easy."

"Do you flame them?"

"Sometimes, but not this morning. I might burn us up."

She looked uncomfortable.

"Anything I can do?"

"You could pour the coffee. I like hot, but not too hot. That's as bad as tepid. It won't be long." I poured some brandy into the cast iron skillet and a small flame shot up and died as quickly. She giggled nervously and lighted a cigarette.

"Mind?"

"Why would I mind? There's an ashtray on the table. Go ahead. I'll be right behind you."

She made a pretty picture seated in the patches of sun

with the room serving as a backdrop for what might have been created for her.

"Good coffee and that looks delicious. No calories? Right?"

Not enough to cause you to worry."

"You were wearing that suit the afternoon we met."

"Was I?"

I closed my eyes and pressed my fingers into my temples. A tangible defeat I could understand, could comfort, but not this which I could not in the least comprehend.

"Yes, with a heavily starched white shirt. White shirts look especially good on you I thought."

"Did you?"

My fairy tale was over. Reality sat opposite me with conversation set on autopilot. Like it does when you've had sex with someone and when it's over you have nothing else to fall back on so you flee as quickly as possible.

"Is the taxi ordered?"

I had scarcely touched my plate. She on the other hand suffered from no lack of appetite. She ate rapaciously.

"Of course. So finish whatever you have to do." I pushed my chair back, getting slowly to my feet. "I'll take care of this."

She rose softly, carefully, dropping her napkin in her empty plate and went from the room. With her gone, I poked at the fire. The flames came leaping to life, curling 'round the logs. I held out my hands for warmth before shoveling on some sand.

Flickering images flashed by my window seat. Her indifference was complete and daunting. I thought what a remarkably unaccommodating presence she possessed and told her so.

"Why? Because I'm a square peg who won't be forced into a round hole? Maybe I'd want a chocolate box cottage life if Mother hadn't made a paean of virtues such as yours and those of your kind. If she hadn't dinned into me 'good old stock! Conservative. Smart. A husband to be proud of and all that—"

"More than that," I cut in. "Tell me, how can you leave Riley to come to me? Come to me when he may have died?"

"No one has squatter's rights on me."

"Then he knew?"

"Of course."

"And he isn't suffering from jealous insanity?"

"Riley's too unrefined for that."

Those words should have stopped me, but I wanted her. I loved her.

"I wanted more than an affair with you," I told her hotly. The woman in the aisle seat with big hair stopped reading and regarded me sympathetically. I blinked her away. "I'm no serial fornicator. I love you. I want to marry you. Spend what's left of my life with you. Hasn't that sunk in or even seeped through?"

Her laugh jeered. When she stopped what she said was spoken with clarity of enunciation.

"Marry you! You're married to yourself."

I was instantly aware of a sickening dropping through space, like hitting an air pocket. I looked into her eyes and the private darkness without her that would be my companion. Her features came back into focus. "I see," I said blankly, feeling a natural death.

I survived grim-faced until I spotted Bud in the tangle of feet at the top of the slow-moving escalator, calling out.

"Why is he calling you that?" she immediately wanted to know.

"It's an affectionate form of address," I answered brusquely.

"How *old* is he?"

"Too *old*, even for you."

"No porter?" his pale face smiled.

"None I could find, Bud."

"Hand them over."

"Not on your life, but would you mind dropping my...my train friend off at her apartment? She lives on South Sixteenth, not far from Racquet."

"Happy to, Miss."

"Thanks," she mumbled.

"You're looking well," he remarked, regarding me curiously.

"But not as trim as you, Bud. Your check-up went well, I gather?"

"Sure did. No cancer to be found."

"I prayed for you."

"I know you did. I did some myself."

"Where am I supposed to sit?" she whispered, as the luggage was being put in the trunk of the nineteen fifty-eight red Sedan Seville whose plush interior is permeated by the smell of Bud's Juicyfruit gum.

"In the back with me. *Where* else?"

The backseat gave us reluctant intimacy, having no hard armrest separating us.

"I drove Mrs. Lammers to the Academy yesterday," Bud was saying.

I stared at the back of the thinning white hair not covered by his cap. As usual, Bud wore the pastel-colored clothes of Palm Beach where he'd once visited.

"How are they all?"

"In the stew you might expect what with the party tonight. Big crowd coming, so I gather. Thought Miss Fox would be with you. She's okay, isn't she?"

"Never better, but she had to go out-of-town on...on business."

"Give her my regards. She's always a sight for these tired old eyes," he chuckled. "She drove up twice to see me when I was in hospital. Did you know that?"

"No, I didn't," I said feeling guilty.

"Well, she did. The first time, she brought me a fruit basket. The biggest one I've ever seen. The nurses said it weighed eighty-five pounds. I couldn't eat it seeing as I had cancer of the jaw and tongue, but it was the thought that counts, and a fine lady like her coming to see me. The second time, Miss Fox brought me a case of gourmet cream soups and some fancy straws. She's a real kind lady. I don't care what some may say. You keep a car in center city, Miss?"

"No, I left it at my parents' when I moved."

"Smart move. Garaging a car in Philly would cost you a pretty penny."

Hearing that compelled me to say, "I'm sorry."

She gave me a quick little smile, "I brought my bicycle."

"Smart move," I repeated.

She opened her bag and scribbled something down.

"This is my new number. Take it, if you want it."

I held it awhile looking at her before putting the folded piece of paper in my pocket.

"Damn," Bud blurted.

"Something wrong?"

"I came down too far. Miss, would you mind walking half a block. You see, I can't make a right. These grid-locked one-way streets will be the death of me."

"Not at all, Bud. I'm sorry to have caused you so much trouble."

"No trouble, Miss. I'm always happy to oblige our friend here."

Bud opened the trunk and I hopped out to hand her her things. The hand that was extended was cold. I felt her breath touch my face.

"I'll call you," she said flatly.

"I hope you will. You know I wish you well."

She crossed to the corner and disappeared like ether, leaving me to return to a succession of tomorrows without her and not even a crumpled love letter to show for my pain.

I was coiled on my bed counting the minutes. Any memories of the party and the rest of the next day were fogged. I made myself answer the phone only when it wouldn't stop ringing.

"You have a collect call from a Miss Calypso Fox," the twangy voice on the other end informed me. "Will you accept the charges?"

"Of course, operator. Calypso?"

My hand shook, a very little.

"I can't talk long. We're not allowed to make or receive

calls. I'm in the director's office. I'm sure she's a dyke. She jabs a
monocle in her left eye, wears safari suits and has close-cropped
blonde hair like Kendall Norris at Foxcroft, except Kendall
wore black hornrims. Her idea of foreplay was forever poking
tennis balls with Miss Bannister the assistant coach. I let Frau
Doktor know fast that while she may like my sofa not to expect
any invitations to sit down. This place is like a concentration
camp. I'd run away, but I couldn't get my money back. One pays
in advance and now I know why. They're starving me to death.
I was given a bottle of mineral water for dinner and locked in
my room when one of the nurses spotted me in the garden
having a cigarette. I tried to bribe a chambermaid to sneak me
in two pints of Hagen Dazs Cookie Dough. She took my money
and laughed. I'm certain they're all certifiable sadists. Are you
laughing at me?"

"Not really. When are you returning?"

"Maybe I should go away more," her tone accused, "but the
reason I called is to find out if you've seen this month's *Town &
Country*?"

"It's somewhere. Why?"

"Owen and Carol are featured. Several pages with color
pictures of their bookstore and apartment. Carol's not an
agent, but they know everyone social and literary in New York.
Carol could sell you. Call her."

Suddenly, I was clear-thinking.

"I will, Calypso. I'll—"

"Ohmygod! That horrid Frau Doktor is coming. Tell Danny
I should have taken her advice. Will you meet my plane?"

"When?"

"I'll write you. Don't take that tone with me, Frau Doktor.
I called collect. It was an emergen—"

She was gone and it would be twelve days before her letter
arrived, and another six before Calypso walked out of Gate 27
at National Airport, looking fit and tanned, and weighing in at
her fighting weight of one hundred and one.

"So you approve of my cleverness," as she called it, Calypso sighed, snuggling closer under the blanket and reaching for my cigarette in the dark on this, the first night of her rapturous return.

"Yep, I owe it all to you. Carol didn't want to take a commission, but I more than insisted. I told her friendship was one thing, but business is business, and it's more of an inducement. She'll get fifteen percent of the book sale. I put it in writing when I wrote to thank her. Sasha kindly delivered the manuscript after I sent her the roundtrip cab fare."

"And Cassandra said the floodgates were going to open, didn't she?" Calypso stretched, giving me back my cigarette.

"So she did."

"So let's go to Bermuda. You need a sabbatical and so do I after my ordeal."

"I don't know, Calypso."

"Well, it can't be money. We're to be houseguests and we did entertain them rather well when they last visited here. Come on," she nudged. "They might invite someone else for next month. We haven't been away for ages. Consider it the beginning of a new career."

Her nails trailed down my chest. "Don't start another cigarette." My mouth was sore from kissing. Had her homecoming brought on this nervous euphoria?

"Calypso," I moaned, "You're insatiable."

When the time came to pack, I brought out the big leather grip from the closet under the stairs and resolutely closed the door on the big yellow patrol boy galoshes that had come from Danny, but not on the fact that I wasn't even considered a 'loose end to be tied up.' For when I'd called the number given me in Philadelphia, I learned from the lease-holder that her young renter had been accepted by the School of Business at Syracuse University and, except for tying up a few loose ends, had moved out.

❧

# Chapter Eighteen

*"Madame no here,"* Esmay informed me in her softest voice, not looking me in the eye as I barged past her stricken face shouting, "Madame is *here*, Esmay. Her phone has been off the hook since we returned from Bermuda, and her car is parked out there on the street."

The first floor was like a vault. If I hadn't known the way I would have had to turn on the lights. Calypso's unpacked grips and purchases remained where Esmay, the driver and I had left them. "I know you're here, Calypso," I yelled, running up the stairs headed for Fitz's fit domain. It is rather dark and gloomy except in the morning and contains innumerable trophies of an athletic and military life. His dress sword hangs above the chimneypiece just below the painting of him with Calypso on his knee. There are two cabinet cases. One containing his medals and another, his collection of intricately carved ivories. In a corner stands a Coromandel screen of some beauty. And, between the windows, a water-colored scroll depicts tortures and execution in the Japanese manner. Photographs line the walls, ships mostly, and foreign ports and of Fitz playing polo in his heyday. Rotting pomegranates in an unpolished trophy bowl today give his lair a mildly acid smell that has displaced the usual scent of the carved camphor-wood temple figures on the bookshelves. Yellowing leather journals recorded in his tight penmanship remain stacked and numbered on the dusty desk top. The hand-knotted Anatolian rug, with its soft, irregular and fading indigo colors, is in need of Hoovering. From the depth of the tortoiseshell tufted leather club chair, from where Fitz, brown as leather from being always out of doors, had read

Asia Minor's ironed newspapers, Calypso regarded me coldly. I'd never felt more closely observed. It came to me with the suddenness and hurt of a blow that in the last months I had done a number of unlikely and distasteful things. I had learned to be deceitful and sly and adroit. I had learned to protect myself. I was soiled with stratagem and evasion and now remorse at seeing what I could do to Calypso, and how easily she could throw off the mantle of reform for liquor-soaked retreat. The unshuttered windows showed her as a blank canvas with no physical warmth. She would be no whiter when she's dead. Her hands twisted around the neck of an unopened bottle of cheap vodka. I caught my breath. She looked down at it, unhappily as a child, and her mouth quivered as if in sorrow over a trivial mishap.

"Calypso," I said uncomfortably.

"Mr. Lonely Hearts," I presume.

I mouthed something, but she swam further out.

"You've made life miserable for me. Go home. Go anywhere." She stopped in agitation and into this hot brooding silence came the rumble of thunder. She rose from the chair, raised her hand and struck me smartly across the mouth.

"And you prate about honor!" She threw her head back in a gesture of Fitz at his best and her jaw was as tenacious. "You said her name in your sleep."

So it was the slip of my subconscious on that penultimate evening that had led us to this less than *intime* state. I moved to hold her and speak soothingly, but she buried her face in her hands and fled at my touch.

"If your bed's a little hard, well, remember you made it." Her lips looked white and stiff. "I know I'm a hag. Go on and say it. I know it. Go to her. Make her your child bride."

Was it then that my love turned apathetic? I didn't know, for there had been no slow death of love, only the slow cancer of disillusionment. I'd gotten what I once prayed for, and I didn't want it. Now I'll serve the rest of my life as her acolyte, lover, keeper. There would be no escape. Only blunted reconciliation and final peace.

"I won't be second best," she screamed, her eyes flying to the portrait painted so long ago. "I won't. I won't. I won't have half loaves. I'll have everything or nothing. I have a right to you. She's young. She doesn't."

"Calypso, shhh, Esmay will hear you. You know that as long as I have a life I will want you. It all begins and ends with you. It always has." I became conscious of a tightness in my throat. "There will be no others."

She swerved away from me, her face alit with fresh anger.

"Tell me," she inquired coldly,—

"There isn't anything to tell, Calypso, she and I just ran out of gas."

She turned her head to protest but collapsed on the window seat and blankly looked out onto the neglected garden. Trap had little time or strength left for getting 'round the borders and the goldfish were gone from the fountain, where a stone boy from Greece rides eternally a golden dolphin. I sat down on the bronze rain drum that wasn't orchestrating our mood in an attempt to derail her growing more dangerously emotional.

"Don't do this to us out of vanity, Calypso. Don't destroy what we had...have for my fantasy of error. I'm sorry. I'm back. I'm staying."

The famous face that had shown classical beauty turned. Her eyes backed down.

"I don't know you anymore. I don't feel anything anymore. I'm terrified. Terrified of everything."

"What makes you think I'm not?"

"You're a man. It doesn't matter. I'm old. People are forgetting. Have forgotten. And I want it back. The Blue Room at the Shoreham. Clothes being sent on approval. My picture in every paper. Remember how Barney Breeskin would stop the band to sing *You're the Top* every time I swept into the Blue Room? Remember how everyone came the night they closed forever and how glum we were? You and Ursula were just back from your honeymoon. How old was I then? You don't have to answer that. I know. That was the night the tall scarecrow in the dirty white linen suit asked me to dance."

We were about to go into our tandem act.

"And I said, 'my husband wouldn't like it'."

"And he said, 'is the asshole passed out your husband'?"

"And I said, 'until the divorce becomes final'."

"And he said, 'then why not marry me'?"

"And I said, 'who are you'?"

"And he said, 'Howard Hughes'."

"And I said, 'who?' He couldn't believe I'd never heard of him, and I told him I only read the parts of the paper that concerned me. But he knew who I was and sent me a year's subscription to the *Evening Star*, the *Daily News* and the *Washington Post*, along with a bushel of orchids. Maybe I should have gone to Hollywood. He did want to put me under contract. However, I didn't like the idea of being owned and he smelled, as I recall."

Tears welled up in her eyes. She was on the verge of a crying jag. She jerked herself back.

"Tony was an asshole, but he was the catch of the season."

"Calypso, stop this, you're not forgotten. *W* wants to do a feature on you, *Town & Country* wants me to write—"

"That's because of that contract with Bergdorf's. It's like I've been rediscovered. Screw them. I'm not about to come back as *Baby Jane* or so that's what became of her after yen, men and alcoholism. And suppose...suppose you come down with..."

"You make it sound like whooping cough, Calypso, when it lasted about as long as a Strauss waltz."

She pulled her cold hands away and fled the room stumbling at my guilt for the safety of her broad soft bed. The swirly floral print of her wide-cut silk beach pajamas made my eyes hurt. I trailed after her carrying the fifth of vodka, passing the life-size portrait of her, commissioned by husband number one. The painting had been executed with dexterity in every tone, the only color being in the hand with its bright new wedding ring. Though the decorations here are as frivolous as the carpentry is solid, there was the faint stale smell of decay beneath the room's general confusion. I reminded her that Bergdorf's would sue if she didn't deliver on schedule. She hunted for a cigarette and blew out a cloud of smoke.

"They wouldn't dare."

"Oh, yes, they would, Calypso, you've taken their money."

"It's more like I've spent their money."

"Well, one thing is certain," I said sitting on the edge of the bed unbidden to fasten the buckle on her T-strap sandal, "they can't sue you if you're dead. Are you trying to break that pretty neck?"

"That Jew buyer of theirs treated me like Grandma Moses. I didn't know anyone in their twenties could be a buyer," she sniffed. "There was a day when the turd would have sold his soul to hang my wrap. I nearly told him that. They do have them, don't they?"

"Have what, Calypso?"

"Souls. I never fully understood."

"Of course they have souls, Calypso. What a question. What they don't believe is that Jesus was the Son of God, only a good rabbi."

"Baby Jesus ended up a rabbi!"

"Calypso," I heaved, "I'm not up to the Trinity. Another time—"

"Where are you going with that bottle?"

"Does it matter?"

She set her stubborn little jaw.

"Do you need it that badly?" I asked in a burst of irritation. "Can't you understand that the song will always be you? When a woman is loved, she is beautiful, Calypso, and I will always see you as young and beautiful. Can't you live off that?"

"Don't lie. I'm a fright. The worry. The pain. The humiliation."

"I've caused you no humiliation, Calypso." I hadn't, for she had flopped and been forgotten by morning."

"If you say so."

"I do say so," I said looking at her wearily.

I would not demean her or myself by saying nothing happened, for everything happened even though it was she who changed her mind.

"Living is incidental without adoration."

I cleared my throat,

"Isn't mine enough?"

She stared at me.

"It...it used to be."

"It still is, Calypso. Don't cry. I'm back and I'll not desert you."

I couldn't. There is nobody to take responsibility for her. Nobody who is interested, much less insisting on having her for a trophy.

"Rest assured, Calypso, there will be no others."

Presently she shook herself.

"And none for me either. It will be like...we're married...and faithful."

She'll live off this for a while and we'll return to sex with nothing else, but that was the price for not having her soul on my conscience.

"Yes, Calypso, like old marrieds who live in separate houses. Hasn't it worked these many years?"

"I...I guess," she admitted falteringly.

I moved fast.

"Oh, this should please you, Calypso. Those first chapters I sent to my friend in New York, he may be interested."

I didn't tell her that my friend thought she was dead.

"He is?" she sniffed.

"Yes, and it's more than a nibble."

"Tell me the truth. Did he remember me or think I was dead?"

"Does it matter, Calypso?"

She wiped her nose on her sleeve.

Tolerantly, I handed her my handkerchief. I've spent my life handing her handkerchiefs.

"I don't want to come back to be forgotten again. And...and as long as you remember."

"Will that be enough, Calypso? Has that ever been enough?"

"It...it...will if you can forget her."

"I can forget her, Calypso."

She wiped her nose again and handed me back my handkerchief.

"So, am I to take it that you're scrapping the book?"

"Not exactly, but I'll not have a humiliating public confession. If your friend is interested in a posthumous autobiography I'll finish it. Having lived well will be my revenge on these young things."

"Whatever you want, Calyso. I'll contact him tommorow about it."

"What about tommorrow?"

"What about it, Calypso?"

"We wasted yesterday. It should have been perfectly obvious that we were made for each other."

And, unfortunately so, it seems.

"Can I be sure about tomorrow?" she asked with dignity.

"*Nous vieillissons n'est-ce pas?* We are getting older, Calypso. The past belongs to our youth without youth's excuses or recoverability. And I...we..." I used the plural, "must learn when to care and not to care. Shall you be all right?"

"I think so."

Without any attempt at a smile, I told her I'd come by later and to get some rest. Rising, I pulled one of the alpaca blankets rescued from the Adirondack sale over her and lightly brushed her cheek with cool lips. She grabbed my hand.

"Tell me, of what are you terrified?" she murmured in a small voice.

"Of many things, Calypso. Of being considered *passe*. Two unsold books and a turn down from Random House."

We were silent for a while.

"Go on," she encouraged, pressing my hand.

"Burnsie buffered me for so long, Calypso, and Carol is an unknown quantity. I've developed high blood pressure and high cholesterol since that operation. There is blood in my urine caused by what Hector terms chronic prostatitis, and, in case you haven't noticed, I've started to gain weight. But most of all, Calypso, I'm terrified of running out of money so late in my life."

"Neither of us would do well poor. From satin to rags isn't funny, but Danny would never let anything happen to you. She'd rob a bank first."

"What's that supposed to mean? That I would let my housekeeper support me?"

"It means that she's in love with you."

"Danny in love with me?"

"The woman would kill for you. God, men. All you really know about love is how to kick it around."

"You've done a lot of kickin' yourself, Calypso."

"So I have, but not anymore. We're going to have the gravy without the ring."

Gravy? Haven't we always? Perhaps that was the problem. She closed her eyes. They were shadowed and Calypso was defenseless with her controlled composure, but I felt nothing but a strong impulse toward pity.

"Calypso, look at me. You don't have any more solutions stashed somewhere, do you?"

I knew my voice sounded dull. I could not make it sound anything else.

She appeared surprised by the question, but shook her head, no.

"Can I trust you, Calypso?"

She lifted her blanched face.

"Why...yes. Yes, you can."

Her voice was like her face, tired, spent. But through it ran a thread, that vibrant cord which linked her to me, that even time itself will not dissolve. I saw her younger. "I can always depend on you," she used to say.

"In that case, I'll see you around eight."

I found Esmay, hunched in a fetal position on the bottom steps covered in the old sable coat Calypso inherited from her mother. She was breathing so quietly that I looked twice to see if she were alive before nuddging her. Her bright dark eyes shot open.

"Madame better?" she inquired anxiously.

"Better, Esmay," I tried to smile, handing her the bottle. She wiped her hands on her sateen apron. "This should stand you well with the trashmen. Call me if Madame has, ah...has a relapse. Do you have my number?"

"Si."

"Good."

Esmay, with her black hair braided to the waist, and her face unpainted, did resemble a convent-reared girl.

"Madame scared child," she said with a sad gap-tooth smile.

This dark girl with the sallow skin and small hard face understood everything.

"Esmay watch her like a mama, si?"

"Si, Esmay. Madame is a child. Has she eaten?"

"She no eat three days. Esmay no leave."

"Are there any eggs?"

"Si."

"Can you poach an egg?"

"Si."

"Well, prepare a tray with two poached eggs and some toast...and some bouillon. Can you do that?"

"Esmay can do."

"Then give Madame a bath and massage. Madame has much work to do. We must keep her well. I'll call back this evening. Thank you, Esmay. Oh, I read recently that talcum powder is good for troubled nerves. Change the linen and sprinkle that or baby powder on the fresh sheets."

"You no leave Madame then?"

"I no leave Madame, Esmay. And it might be a good idea to open the curtains. It's like a tomb in here."

"Si," she nodded, pulling the knitted shawl closely to her as she walked me to the door.

"Madame is lucky to have you Esmay."

"Esmay never leave Madame."

"Can I depend on that?" I turned, my hand on the doorknob. Would this peasant girl be strong enough? "That is if something should happen to me, Esmay?"

"No worry, sir, Esmay no leave Madame."

I patted her shoulder and closed the door on what was, for I left knowing what love had done to me. Love, which should have made me free and honest and finer had made me the exact opposite. I'd become a liar and a cheat. I had wanted to love again and in doing so confused this desperate need with love itself. Now I would put a hopeless love out of my life, fully knowing that what I was going to do would be forever irreversible. For the day had come. The day I would call Syracuse. How many times had I replayed what I would say? The first leaves were appearing almost by surprise and it seemed only yesterday that Danny had laid in the winter flannel boxers. The false brightness of Sunday fled. The weather was about to pull another tantrum, perhaps more violent than yesterday's storm. Blood pulsed hotly in my forehead. Not once did I think that she would not be there when I dialed. Block after block I walked toward the Hill, not taking M Street to Pennsylvania Avenue and out, but Dumbarton to P Street across Dupont Circle and out Massachusetts Avenue where some semblance of order still carries over. The world is emptying. It won't last my lifetime. Georgetown is in shambles and Dupont Circle worse. My grandparents must be spinning in their graves. My parents as well. Clarence Moore was lucky. He went down on the *Titanic* and was saved seeing the house he built for his bride empty with soggy mattresses piled at the weedy curb along with other refuse. I counted church bells and was consumed with the desire to wound. Taxis slowed and tooted. I shook my head and they passed me wondering, for the rain pissed down and I didn't increase my pace, only continued unhurried and uncaring of health or clothes and burning for vindication. After awhile I was the only person out, even the homeless had found shelter. Four miles I walked with rivulets running under my shirt collar and behind my contact lenses, my Weejuns making squishy sounds. The wind came up. My red poplin pants glued to my legs and my crew neck sweater became a millstone. A silver car whipped past me going near eighty and I wasn't bothered enough to give an angry glare. I felt on the attack as my house neared and paused only to latch the gate behind me. With back straight and shoulders squared I let myself in and went up the twenty-three steps to the study where I poured a stiff whiskey and threw the cushiony wool horse blanket, the one with black, orange and red stripes, over the chair before sitting down. I dialed without having to look at the back of the envelope on which the number was written. She picked up on the sixth ring, demanding, "Who is this?"

"You're obviously not on velvet, so it must have been some party, seeing it's going on two."

I prided myself on the ease of my opening and swigged down some whiskey, dripping dampness.

"Oh, it's you," was the best she could do.

I lighted a cigarette.

"You sound overjoyed."

She yawned uncomfortably.

"How did you get my number?"

"By dialing 315-555-1212."

"That cost you a dollar."

"It would have been cheap at twice the price. I gather you're having fun being back *behind* the walls of ivy."

"Fun! You're...well, you're you. I'm putting in sixty or more hours a week between studying and going to class. I've been up all night cramming."

"Best be careful. All work and no play will make you a dull girl. Did you get my card from Bermuda?"

"I think so."

"You receive that many postcards from Bermuda?"

"Yes, I received it. So who are the Dill's?"

"The friends with whom Calypso and I stayed. Splendid house, *Edey's Hill*. Been in the family going on two hundred years. Spectacular sea views and an 1880's gazebo for languid afternoon teas, G&T's and quiet reads."

"Funny name, Dill."

"Diana Dill is David's aunt."

"Who cares?"

"I imagine Kirk Douglas's children do. She's their mother."

I lifted my glass, toasted myself and waited. When nothing came, I offhandedly inquired, "How's what's his name? The one with cancer? Are you in widow's weeds or only wearing a black band on your sleeve?"

Her breathing was becoming heavy.

"Riley's fine. He worried for nothing."

"I could have told you only the good die young."

"Is that why you called?"

"No, I called because you never thanked me."

"It was getting too serious. So I—"

"On whose part?"

"That's the way it was done to me."

"By whom? Eros?"

"Yes, Eros."

"That's a relief. I thought perhaps it was because you were intimidated."

"By who...whom?" she self-corrected, taking the bait.

"By the dance. Sulgrave."

"What did *they* say?"

"Oh, little things. Nothing I can recall."

"Not even one?"

She was wide, wide awake.

"Let's see. Was it Henry—?"

"Who?"

"Henry. Margaret's husband."

"Oh."

"Well, Henry did wonder why I would bring a girl to a dance who didn't know how to dance."

"What did you say?"

"The truth. That I hadn't known. I'd assumed any properly-reared young person from Chestnut Hill danced. Even one deprived of dancing classes."

I waited, knowing she would want me to continue.

"Nothing else?"

"Not, really. Oh, no one knew your people or why you weren't married, or, ah...what year you came out. But all that's neither here nor there for they have forgotten you. The main thing is you never thanked me."

"That's not my style."

"That's *not* style," I contradicted sharply. It's no style. It's plain bad manners and that you're building a life on no foundation I could not care less."

My acid speech was meant to be acid, delivered with shrewd self-preservation behind every word, and I really hit.

She said uncertainly, "Caroline remembers me."

"No, she doesn't. I lied to you. Never once has Caroline ever breathed your name. I called and asked her to come by as a special favor and act as if she remembered you." I felt chilly and my teeth were about to chatter. I took another swig. "And since you never had the manners to say goodbye, I will, 'Goodbye,'" I said, dropping the heavy black earpiece on anything she might have said. My chill increased. I ignored it. Instead, I crushed out what was left of the stub of my cigarette, opened the middle drawer and pulled out a new yellow-lined legal tablet. Slapping it down on the desk, I removed the cap from a new black felt-tip pen. Amanda had said I was living a new book. Well, when she said that, she'd been correct. Today though, I had lived a new book. *She Came of Decent People* would do as a working title. The main thing was I wanted to portray her with coldhearted lucidity and compassion. Perhaps it would be my salvation. It might give me back my career. The chiming mechanism in the grandfather clock whirred itself into action and struck off the hour. Danny would soon be coming home. And just like the line in T.S. Eliot's *Little Gidding*, "Dust in the air suspended marks the place where the story ended."

࠾